LOVER'S SACRIFCE

ASHLEY WEBSTER

Lover's Sacrifice

Friend's To Lover's, Volume 1

Ashley Webster

Published by Ashley Webster, 2022.

LOVER'S SACRIFICE

First edition. June 22, 2022.

Copyright © 2022 Ashley Webster.

ISBN: 979-8223368786

Written by Ashley Webster.

Table of Contents

I dedicate this book to my two daughters. Becoming their mom will always be the greatest gift I have ever been given. Writing a book is something I was always afraid to do, but with their love and undying faith in me, I knew I needed to be brave and show them that just because something is scary, it does not mean it is not worthwhile. I love you girls and I hope to make you as proud of me as I am of you.

PROLOGUE

(MADDIE)

The summer sun shines as I sit in my favorite meadow behind our high school. I cannot believe I am entering into my senior year already.

I'm sitting here watching the breeze blow my favorite yellow wildflowers as I wait for my best friend, Lucas and I cannot help but wonder if this will be the year he finally sees me as something more than his childhood best friend.

I have been in love with Lucas since I was six years old. I met him when I moved into the house next door. I know, how cliché am I wanting him to fall in love with the girl next door?

Lucas is the quarterback of the football team. He has led his team to state championships since his freshman year. The first freshman of Boyd High School to make starting quarterback.

He's popular while I am a nerd, always with my head in a book, but somehow, we have managed to stay best friends, even if the cheerleaders hate me for it.

The sun is starting to set, and I cannot help wondering if Lucas forgot about me.

It has been our ritual since as long as I can remember that we meet here the night before the first day of school.

We talk about our goals for the year and our dreams while spending the evening laughing and running through the meadow.

The fact that it is the night before senior year is not lost on me. This will be our last time to meet here like this and predict how the year will go and that honestly makes me quite sad, which does not make my disappointment that he seems to have forgotten any better.

Maybe this is the beginning to the end? He and I are planning to attend different colleges. I am heading off to NYU, if I get in, and he will go wherever his football carries him.

While I sit here lost in my thoughts and enjoying the breeze, suddenly his arms are wrapped around me in a tight embrace and internally I swoon.

His wonderful cologne he started wearing a few months ago fills me with warmth. He smells like leather and spice, and it is a scent permanently etched into my brain and fills me with comfort.

"Sorry, I'm late," he says softly and with his arms around me like this, I can feel his warm breath on my ear which fills my stomach with butterflies.

My head lifts and I look into his crystal-clear blue eyes and smile. His dark hair is messy and longer than normal for him making the front fall over his eyes. He is wearing his red team tee shirt and black basketball shorts. His black chucks finishing his comfortable ensemble. His small freckles on his nose add to his charm and his jaw is impossibly chiseled for a highschooler. He is all lean muscle and at least a foot taller than me. His tanned skin glows in this light and he exudes confidence wherever he goes. Is it really a question why I am head over heels for him?

"It's okay," I mumble. "I haven't waited long." I lie through my teeth.

He doesn't need to know I thought he forgot me. He sits down beside me and stares out into the meadow. It really is quite the view at sunset. With the sky filled with colorful rays and the wildflowers swaying in the breeze, it is almost romantic. These moments out here with him always feel like a special date and mean so much to me even if that isn't what they are.

As we sit side by side in silence, I notice he is fidgeting, something he only does when he is nervous and Lucas does not get nervous so it makes no sense.

"Hey Maddie?" There is a slight tremble to his voice and that sets me on edge. "Can I ask you something?" I smile up at him in hopes of easing his nerves and in an attempt to calm myself down. It doesn't work.

"What's up Lucas?" I watch him as he continues to fiddle and squirm around. The minute that passes seems like hours. He takes a deep breath and blurts, "Do you think you could ever see yourself dating me?" His eyes show he is terrified of my answer and his fidgeting increases. Is his breathing unsteady?

I am stunned into silence; I am pretty sure my mouth falls wide open. Never in a million years would I have thought he would ever see me as anything more than a friend, but maybe he doesn't and is asking as more of an open-ended thing. Maybe he is interested in someone and wants to know if he is likeable or something.

"Lucas, any girl would be beyond lucky to be with you." I finally get out with a shaky voice. That answer that won't give away the fact that I love him at least. Not really sure where to go from here, considering I am still shocked to the core, I sit, wait, and watch him while holding my breath waiting to see where he is going with this. Worst case scenario, I am about to hear about his latest love interest and need to be prepared to act normal. Too bad my acting skills are subpar.

"Maddie, I have had this crush on you for a while now. I have been afraid to tell you and ruin our friendship, because what we have is so special to me." He looks down at my hands as I hold them tightly together and deflates a little bit. I am too scared to say a word.

He stops and shakes his head and takes a deep breath and puts his shoulders back exuding his normal confidence once again. "I would like to take you on a date and maybe you could" He looks around nervously letting his confident mask slip before taking back control and saying, "be my girlfriend at some point?"

I don't even have time to think about what I am doing.

Suddenly my arms are around him and I am smiling so much it hurts. When I pull back, he smiles at me and slowly comes forward. "Can I take that as a yes?" He says with a cocky smirk.

This is the moment I have dreamed about since I met him and I can't believe my first kiss is going to be with him. This is exactly how I dreamt it would be and why I am a senior and have never been kissed. I wanted all of my firsts to be special and no one else could compare to him.

As his lips meet mine gently, I just know in my heart that Lucas Andrews is going to be my forever. He owns my heart, even if he doesn't know it yet. He has had it for years.

Little did I know, this would be the beginning of the end for Lucas and me. A beautiful beginning with a tragic end. The universe has a funny way of ruining everything and I am about to learn that lesson the hard way.

CHAPTER ONE

(MADDIE)

8 months later

I can't believe we have three weeks left of senior year and prom is already here. Time is going by so fast.

Senior year has been a dream. Lucas and I are celebrating our eight-month anniversary and it just so happens' to be prom night too. This is going to be the most romantic night ever. I can't think of a better way to celebrate. Last week, Lucas told me he loved me. It felt so good to finally hear the words I have felt for as long as I can remember.

Of course, I cried a little and said it back and he teased me about being emotional. Our friendship is the foundation that makes us work so well and leads to endless teasing of one another. I highly recommend falling in love with your best friend.

Not that we haven't had many battles along the way. Him being so popular means all the girls throwing themselves at him all the time, which drives me insane, might I add. Then there is me, and I am so focused on my studies and getting into NYU that I drive him crazy, because more of our dates are study dates than actual dates, but somehow, we make it work and never fight with one another, which is pretty amazing if I do say so myself.

Though this time is exciting, I am dreading him taking off to play for OU in the fall and me heading to NYU. I don't know how we are going to handle long distance; I just know we both want to handle it and stay together.

Lucas has a surprise for me tonight and I cannot wait to find out what it is. I have a feeling I am going to lose my virginity tonight and for the first time ever, I truly feel ready to take that step with Lucas.

I went and had my hair done at my mom's friend Maggie's salon down the street and of course she gave me the royal treatment and I ended up getting my nails done as well by her cousin, Betty. My hair is up in some sort of twisted bun with curls framing my face and my nails are white, because they assured me it was a classic, I could not beat and would look amazing with my dress. I am finishing the final touches to my make-up, which I rarely wear, but I am going all out for tonight. I want everything to be perfect.

My mom knocks on my door as I am finishing my make-up and bursts in with excitement. She is so extra sometimes.

"Oh, my goodness, Maddie. You truly look stunning!" she says with a radiant smile. She saves this smile just for me. She is one of my closest friends. She is an amazing mom and always puts me first.

She is beautiful too. She has always been into makeup and fashion and loves it when I get dressed up, rather than stick to my jeans, chucks, and tee shirts I normally wear. I drive her bonkers with how laid back I am with my appearance. She is always saying how I am only young once and to do it up right. But she loves me, even in a tee shirt.

"Thank you, mom, I'm so excited for tonight," I respond and can hear the excitement in my own voice. I really am looking forward to this!

I wonder if it would be weird to talk to my mom about the possibility of losing my virginity tonight. Deep down I know I can tell her anything and normally tell her everything. Guess that makes the decision for me right there. She would want to know this anyways.

"Mom, can I talk to you about something?" I know she can hear the nervousness in my voice when she lowers her brows and puckers her lips like she always does when something is bothering me or she knows I am going to say something she doesn't like. Oh well, here goes nothing.

"Of course, baby," she says in that understanding and sweet tone she always has. It's annoying sometimes how calm and collected she is when I am always a mess. I take a deep breath and just let it out in a rush.

"Mom, I think I am going to have sex with Lucas tonight." I close my eyes and wait and don't even realize I am holding my breath until she puts her hand on my knee and when I open my eyes, she has a smile on her lips. See, always freakishly understanding.

"Baby, I know I can't say anything to stop you and I know you love Lucas, but please be safe and make sure you are truly ready. Your virginity isn't something you can get back once it is gone," she has a look of concern, but is still smiling at me so I know this isn't an easy conversation, but one she is ready to have with me.

I take a second to think about what she said and know in my heart, no one else in this world could compare to Lucas Andrews and I want him to have all my firsts.

"Mom, I am still taking my pill every day. You put me on it the second I started dating him. I am safe and I know I am ready, and he is who I want to experience this with. I want to experience all of my firsts with him." I assure her. My mom smiles at me, and I notice a single tear has fallen down her cheek and move to wipe it away.

"My baby is growing up. You'll be leaving home soon. Thank you for not being too old to still share things with me. Remember, I am always here for you," she says with a hint of sadness to her tone. I know she is dreading me leaving, especially for New York.

With that, she leaves me to put my dress on. I chose a royal blue color. It is strapless and tight through the bodice, before flowing down to the ground. It is satin and just beautiful, like Lucas's eyes. It has beads lining the top and has a plunging back that stops just above my tailbone. The top has a slight dip between my breasts and because it is so tight and has a built-in push up bra, it makes my boobs look amazing. I bought a matching lace thong to go underneath in case we do decide tonight is the night. I slip on my white sparkly pumps with a royal blue bottom my mom surprised me with to go with my dress. I take a final look in the mirror and can't fight the smile from my lips. "Tonight is going to be magical." I whisper to myself.

I hear the doorbell and head downstairs to greet him. Of course, my mom feels the need to take a million pictures before we can leave in his red mustang. I will never forget his face when he got it for his eighteenth birthday. It was the highlight of our junior year, and I didn't have to take the bus anymore, because he has picked me up every day since. Lucas and I don't even get to exchange hellos before she has us posing for pictures.

"Mom, I love you, but we have to go now and you have at least a million pictures to choose from." I say finished with the constant flashing.

"Will you send those to me?" Lucas asks her with his signature smile in place, not showing his announce in the slightest.

"Of course, I will sweetie. You two have fun and please be careful." My mom says and leans in to kiss my forehead and then turn and hug Lucas.

As we head to the car, Lucas plants a gentle kiss on my lips. "You are beautiful, Maddie."

"Thank you, babe" I say with a smile after returning his kiss.

AC/DC is playing in the car. Lucas is a huge fan of classic rock. It is always his go to music. We cruise along in silence while holding hands and stealing glances as one another. He is all smiles and making me even more excited for my surprise. I have no idea what he has planned, but I know it will be amazing.

We arrive at prom a few minutes later and Lucas lets go of my hand after giving it a gentle kiss and heading around the car to open my door for me. We head inside and as soon as we walk in we are hit with beauty.

My friend Sarah is on the prom committee and did an amazing job with her planning committee. Sarah is super bubbly and fun and always the life of the party. She is the complete opposite to my shy and quiet side. But hey, opposites attack right?

The theme is Paris Nights and gorgeous is an understatement. Paris is the city of love, and there are twinkling lights everywhere, an Eiffel Tower, and she even got a band to play live music. She has flowers everywhere and it really does have a Paris feel and screams romance and beauty. Everything is soft tones and elegance. The table clothes are satin. The lights are low and set the mood. I can't believe she did all this on the school budget.

We dance, we sing, and we have a blast with our friends throughout the night. Which is a huge accomplishment since we come from different social circles, which seem to have come together for the night. Every slow song is bliss. Lucas holds me tightly and we sway to the music. The only complain I have is that everyone keeps staring at me.

It truly seems like everyone is in on this surprise and knows something is coming and they all keep looking at me in anticipation.

Everything is truly perfect, besides that. I love Lucas, but if he doesn't get on with this soon, I am going to lose my mind. Or at least tell everyone to stare at someone else already.

Sarah is wearing a gorgeous pink lacey dress and her blonde hair is cascading down her back in curls. Her freckles are on full displace, but here eye make-up has a dramatic wing to it that makes it all pop. She planned all this and still managed to have time to look like a goddess. I am so proud of her. She gracefully walks onto the stage, looking like a princess, and announces it is time to crown the king and queen.

This is the only part of prom I was dreading. Lucas knows me well and drapes his arm around me, because this means my superstar boyfriend has to hang with the new queen for a portion of our night.

"It is going to be okay." His warm breath fans my ear as he whispers to me, which sends chills down my spine in the best way.

"Easy for you to say, you are going to be prom king! I am the one who will have to watch you dance with Kate," I say annoyed. We all know that Kate will be crowned and it makes me sick.

Kate is this obnoxious, slutty, cheerleader. Captain to be exact. Her and I have always hated one another. She has spent the entire year trying to get Lucas to leave me for her. Captain of the cheer squad should be with the quarterback, right? Cliché and stupid if you ask me...

Why does this have to be a part of our perfect night? I trust Lucas completely, but I hate her hands on him in anyway, because I know she would jump at the chance to get in his pants and screw me over. She's just mad that I am top of our class and after this, her glory days are over, but regardless, Lucas is my man, and I won't have her ruin my night.

"Listen, I am going to refuse to dance with her and come find my true queen. So, you have nothing to worry about, babe," he says it like it's no big thing. You can't leave the queen and skip the king and queen dance. This crazy boyfriend of mine.

As if she would ever let that happen anyways and miss a chance to get her hands on my man. But I am not going to say that and ruin his moment so instead smile and kiss his cheek.

Sarah grabs the microphone again and begins speaking, "I am honored to crown my best friend's man as king! Lucas Andrews, can you make your way to the stage for me so I can crown your annoying self?" she says with a gleam in her eyes.

What is she up too? He kisses my cheek and heads to the stage as everyone claps and he is crowned king. Look at him up there. I am the luckiest girl in the world, because he is the hottest guy in this whole school.

"Thank you, guys, for voting for me and making high school amazing, but the biggest thanks goes to my wonderful girlfriend, Maddie," he says with adoration causing the crowd to clap louder. He is so perfect.

I swoon at his sweetness and forget why I was frazzled and upset to begin with. Lucas has never given me a reason to doubt him. So, I refuse to start now and let Kate ruin any part of prom for us.

"Now, since Sarah has allowed me the honor, can my queen please come join me on the stage? Maddie Wilson, get up here and kiss your king!" he says with total confidence.

Everyone starts cheering and I am left standing there in shock with my mouth wide open and of course the spotlight chooses that moment to find me. Did he just ask me to come stand with him as his queen? He can't do that. We have to vote for it. There is no way I won.

Man, Kate is going to be so upset. I make my way up to the stage and into his waiting arms. Suddenly a crown is placed on my head. I turn my head and Sarah is smiling at me and her eyes look glassy like she is fighting back tears.

"Let's hear it for Maddie Wilson, our prom queen!" She exclaims and throws her hands out to showcase me. "The prettiest one we have ever had, but I am her bestie so I am biased!" She shouts for everyone to hear.

As Sarah says the words, Kate marches onto the stage in a fit of rage and starts trying to snatch my crown off my head like the total bitch she is. Way to ruin the moment...

"This is mine!!! They rigged it to be together! It's mine!" She is going nuts and being laughed at by the entire prom in the process. The microphone is picking up her entire fit. She is even stomping like a toddler. I am having to fight the urge to laugh as Lucas shields me from her wrath.

Principle Tate interferes and steers her toward the exist while whispering things I can't hear, but I am proud of myself for not making a single comment during her entire tantrum. Once she is outside, the cheers begin for my king and myself again and this time they are chanting for us to dance.

"Shall we dance Miss Wilson?" Lucas has his hand extended for me to take and I not only take it, but I hold on tight.

We make our way to the dance floor where the music begins, and everyone claps for us.

"How on earth did this happen?" I know I have to ask and make sure Kate is wrong and that he didn't rigged the vote.

"Duh, silly girl. We are the couple everyone loves and cheers for. I nominated you and of course everyone voted for the true queen." My heart is bursting at the seams. This really just happened. I am prom queen.

How did I get so lucky? I get to be in love with my best friend. My other best friend is incredible. I am going to NYU in the fall. Everything is just so perfect.

Prom is ending and we are heading to the car when Lucas stops me and asks, "Hey Maddie, why don't we go sit in our meadow before we go? This night has been so perfect, and we should at least spend part of it in our special place where we began." He is so right, the perfect end to our prom and eight-month anniversary is to go to our meadow, where it all began.

When we make it to the back of the school and head down to the meadow, I notice he has set up a blanket with a picnic basket and lantern. As we get comfortable on the blanket I say "Lucas, this is so perfect. Thank you for doing all this for me."

"Of course, baby. I wanted this night to be perfect for you in every way." His signature smirk is in place, and it warms my heart. "What is in that pretty head, gorgeous."

I look up and find him smiling down at me, his eyes sparkling in the pale moonlight. "Kiss me." These two little words are the sweet beginning to the best kiss of my life. Sparks fly and I know this is about to be a moment I never forget.

CHAPTER TWO

(LUCAS)

Sitting here kissing my girl under the stars is amazing, but I can't help but feel guilty that I have not told her I am graduating early and leaving for OU sooner than expected. OU's quarterback broke his arm, and they need me sooner rather than later. Which means our summer plans are out the window and everything is about to change. Thank god I have all my credits and can graduate early.

I pull back and stare into her eyes. She is smiling and so happy.

Maybe tonight isn't the night to tell her.

It has been so perfect, and it will only ruin it, but I am running out of time. I leave tomorrow morning. I am in my thoughts when I notice she is unbuttoning my shirt slowly. "Maddie, what are you doing?" I say with trepidation.

"Lucas, you have been so patient with me. You never once pressured me. Thank you for that, but I am ready now and want to end this perfect night by giving you every piece of me," she says with love in her eyes and a voice that sounds sultrier than I have ever heard from her.

My heart is racing. I love her so much. All my earlier thoughts wash away and disappear as I hold her and start kissing her again. That is going to have to wait.

She finishes with my buttons and pushes my blue shirt off my shoulders.

I unzip her dress while kissing her slowly down her neck. The soft moan she lets out causes my dick to stir in my pants and strain against the zipper.

She's left standing in these beautiful blue lace panties and her fuck me heels. I lay my shirt out on the ground and ease her down to lay back on it to give her extra padding. The blanket I brought is soft, but I want her to be as comfortable as possible. I lift her leg and slide off her high heel before lifted the other to do the same gently rubbing her feet in the process. I lean forward and kiss her again. She fumbles with my belt while I kiss down her collarbone and caress her breasts. Her nipples come to attention instantly and she moans softly with each tinder touch. Her breasts are perfect and fit in my hand like they were made for them.

She uses her feet to push my pants and boxers down together and instantly reaches for my throbbing cock. She starts stroking hard as I make my way down to her nipples and suck one into my mouth while playing with the other one in my hand. The moan she lets our makes me grow in her palm. I spend a long time worshipping her breasts and leaving marks on each one.

I work my way down her body, forcing her to release my cock from her amazing strokes. I make eye contact with her as I lower closer to her core.

"Are you sure you are ready? We can stop," I try to get out with strength in my voice, but I know I sound huskier than normal, and it would take great restraint to stop at this point, but I would for her in a heartbeat.

"Please don't stop Lucas. I am ready. I am so ready," she says eagerly while pushing me closer to my destination.

With that, I lower my head and suck directly on her clit. She squirms and squeals beneath me as I slide in one finger. I almost took the time to tease her, but the second she started pulling me closer, I knew I made the right call. This is further than we have ever gone before. She tastes so sweet. Nothing I have ever tasted is this wonderful. I add one on my fingers and use her wetness to slip it inside and she lets out a strangled cry of pleasure, so I add another finger and curve my fingers to really hit the right spot.

"Lucas, please, make love to me," she cried out and it comes out all breathlessly. She begs while bucking under me and urging my fingers on with gentle thrusts. I refuse to stop before she comes though. I work her harder and push my fingers out with abandon. I bit down on her clit and it pushed her over the edge and I have to use my free hand to hold her in place. Once she settles, I climb up and kiss her lips and let her taste herself, which earns me another moan. "Are you sure you are ready?"

I have to ask one final time and make sure, she is positive before I take her virginity. She lets out a loud breath, "Lucas please."

And that's the moment it hits me that I don't have a condom. I did not come prepared or stay prepared, because I did not want that to be an added pressure for her at any point and time.

"Maddie, I don't have a condom. I just didn't plan for this. I didn't want to carry one and pressure you," I can hear the defeat in my own tone.

This sucks so much. I hang my head and try to gain control of my breathing preparing to stop what we are doing. I feel so stupid. Way to be unprepared Andrews.

"Lucas, I am on the pill. It's okay," again she says breathily causing my cock to stir even more.

The second the words are spoken; I am at her entrance without hesitation. I know I need to go slow with her and probably should not take the risk, but in this moment, nothing else matters.

I move in slowly. She lets out a wince, so I give her a moment to adjust and kiss down her neck, but she quietly begins to moan in my ear and beg me to move.

I kiss her deeply, letting our tongues dance as they were always meant to and begin to move slowly inside of her while kissing her deeply. She slowly starts to match my pace and we move in sync with one another. I can feel it building and she begins to clench down on me. We move slowly but in sync together for what feels like forever.

"I am going to come." I warn breathlessly.

"Come Lucas!" she screams and just like that we come together in total ecstasy.

I see stars and not the ones in the sky. But now that it's over and I am holding her, guilt consumes me, because I know I am about to shatter her and break her heart when I tell her I am leaving.

CHAPTER THREE

(MADDIE)

The moon is shining down on us as I stroke his back and he lays beside me. I have just experienced my first two orgasms and given my virginity to the boy who holds my heart. It has been the most perfect night of my life.

"I love you, Lucas." It comes out quiet as a prayer, but he wraps his arms around me and whispers, "I love you more, but are you sure you are, okay?" again with trepidation in his voice.

Doesn't he see how happy I am right now? "I am more than okay so stop asking and ruining the moment." I say and put all my sass into it.

I feel the shift in him. Something is bothering him. "Lucas, what's wrong?" I ask in a panicked voice. "Was it bad for you?" It being my first time, I am flooded with fears that it was not good for him, and he just doesn't want to tell me I am bad at sex. Shit.

"Listen, I have to tell you something and you aren't going to like it." He looks beyond guilty right now and it is scaring me.

Oh, no. I was right. I was awful at sex and he never wants to have sex with me again. I can feel myself on the brink of an anxiety attack. At least I think that is what this is, because I have never had one before.

"I am leaving tomorrow for OU," he says sadly and looks down at his hands. I can't have just heard him, right? School isn't even over yet.

"What are you even talking about, we have three weeks left of school and graduation, and all summer before we have to be separated."

His face is filled with emotion and his eyes shine with unshed tears. "Maddie, OU's quarterback broke his arm. You know their back-up quarterback flunked out three months ago. They need me now. It's all been worked out for me to graduate early and leave. I am so sorry I didn't tell you. I didn't want to ruin our anniversary and prom. Please don't be mad. We can call, text, facetime, and still be together," he says in a panic. "We always knew we had to be separated for a while, it is just coming a little earlier than we thought, but I love you and this doesn't change anything for me."

All the euphoria I was feeling moments ago shatters like glass. He is leaving...tomorrow? But he is my best friend, the love of my life. We knew we had to be separated, he is right about that, but we still had months to figure out how to make long distance work.

All these thoughts are overwhelming my brain, but when I look into his eyes, I know what he needs me to do. I can see the turmoil he is in and I know how to make this better.

He is afraid and in pain, so I say the only words I can, because nothing matters to me more than him.

"Lucas, we are going to be alright. It's us against the world, okay?"

With that, he lets out a huge sign and he kisses me. We hear people in the distance and hurry and get dressed. It's time to go home and tomorrow, I will have to say goodbye and I truly just don't know how I can. I need to try to enjoy the little bit of time I have left with him tonight and worry about the rest tomorrow.

CHAPTER FOUR

(MADDIE)

I swear I have tossed and turned all night.

I can see the sun peeking through my window, which means morning has come for me. How am I going to say goodbye to Lucas today? After our magical night, this just seems so unfair.

I know this is something he needs to do. It is for his career. It has always been his dream to play in the NFL and this is a steppingstone in that direction, but why does his dream have to hurt so badly?

Here I am complaining... I got into OU. It was my back up school, but when I got into NYU, I made the choice to go there and never even told him about it.

I wanted to study journalism and NYU was the better choice for me. I could have put him first and chosen to go to OU, but mu dream was to go to NYU so who am I to complain about him following his dreams and it hurting me. I know this is going to hurt him to. Being apart will suck, but we are strong and will make it work.

My mom is clearly awake, I can smell the coffee all the way up here. I force myself out of bed and make my way downstairs. My mom was asleep by the time I got home last night, and I didn't get to see her or tell her the news. Not about me losing my virginity or about Lucas leaving. This ought to be fun.

"Good morning, Mom." I try to speak as normally as possible, but I know my tone shows my mood. Of course, my mom picks up on that right away because she has some freaky radar and knows everything. It is weird to say the least.

"Are you okay? Are you regretting having sex? Did you have sex?" she questions rapidly.

Wow, okay, she assumes it has something to do with that. Well here goes nothing I guess.

"Yes, mom. I lost my virginity. And, it was the most romantic and wonderful night of my life," I respond in a hushed tone.

"I can't say that excites me, but I am happy it was a positive experience for you. If nothing is wrong having to do with that, then what's the matter?" Her brows are drawn again, and you can see the concern on her face.

I sigh and hate even having to say the words. "Lucas has to leave for OU today," I state feeling defeated. The gasp she lets out surprises me.

"You mean to tell me that he slept with you and has to leave the very next day? What a piece of..." I can't even hold in my anger at this point and cut her off.

"HE IS A WONDERFUL GUY, MOM!!" I know I am yelling, but how could she think he did anything wrong? "This is out of his control. Their quarterback broke his arm, and they need him now. It isn't his fault. I wanted last night to happen, and I am glad it did."

My mom looks shocked, probably because I have never yelled at her before. We have a good relationship and do not argue or yell at one another. My mom is taking some deep breaths and I can tell she is reining herself in.

"Maddie, I am sorry this is happening and that I assumed he used you before he left, but I still do not think he should have slept with you knowing he had to leave. I know this can't be easy for you and I am here for you if you need to talk. I think it is best if I go out for my morning run. Give you a moment to cool off before you end up ground for life. But if you need to talk and can do so calmly, I will stay." I hang my head low.

"No, Mom, you go ahead and go. You are right, my emotions are all over the place and now isn't the time to talk, but I will need you when I get back from saying goodbye to him."

She shakes her head. "I know this isn't easy baby, but I also know you are a strong girl with a bright future, and everything will work out as it should. I love you." She turns to head for the door, but I stop her and grab her arm.

"I am sorry, Mom. I love you too."

"You don't get to disrespect me, but I understand just this one time." She hugs me tightly and then she heads out the door, leaving me standing here feeling awful for speaking to her that way.

I head back upstairs to shower and get ready to go see Lucas before he leaves with my head hung low. I never fight with my mom and disrespect her like that. I am in my feels and to top it off have to say goodbye to Lucas and just can't get my emotions under control. OU is about four hours away. It is not like we can't visit, but this still sucks. How can this work?

Maybe I can go see him on the weekends or something before I head to NYU. Yeah, that's it, I need to try to think positively and not go down this road and convince myself it is going to fail.

The warm water helped to release the tension from my fight with my mom, but it is doing nothing to make me hate this day less. I don't know how to say goodbye. I just want to curl up with him and keep him here.

I opted to skip make up since I will likely cry during this goodbye. I put on jeans and a rock band tee shirt and reached for my vans so I would at least be comfortable for this hell.

Now I am out the door with my hair falling in natural waves the way Lucas likes it and still damp from my shower. He loves my brunette waves and has made a point to ensure I know it. I drive a brand-new Honda Civic, nothing fancy, but my dad bought it for me.

Guess he felt bad for not being around while I was growing up and thought he should send something to rejoice in the fact that I am now eighteen and child support ends for him. Maybe that is why this is so hard for me. I am used to men leaving and not coming back because they choose their secretary over their family.

Note to self, Lucas is not like that, and I need to wipe that from my mind.

Normally, I would just walk next door, but we decided to meet in our meadow, which now holds every special memory we have ever had. Well, the important ones anyways. The drive isn't long and when I park and walk around to the back of school where the meadow is I spot him, sitting in our special spot. He is looking at the wildflowers and seems deep in thought. I have to pause and let memories wash over me.

This is where we shared our first kiss and decided to be more than friends.

This is where we sat when my dad left six years ago, and he was the glue that held me together so I could be strong for my mom.

This is where we planned our schoolyears and made predictions for every year before the first day of school.

This is where we fell in love and made love for the first time.

This is where we grew up and grew together as best friends and got to know each other.

This will always be our special place.

As I make my way toward him, I notice that he is not alone.

Kate is right in front of him. What is she doing here? I am about halfway to him when my whole world comes crashing down all around me. Kate is leaning in. Everything feels as if it is moving in slow motion. And then her lips find his and I swear this is the moment my heart stopped beating before shattering into a million pieces. This can't be real life right now. The tears are already streaming down my face.

CHAPTER FIVE

(LUCAS)

I decided to get to the meadow early.

I wanted a moment to reflect on the many memories that Maddie and I shared here. This is the spot where I gave her my heart, repeatedly and to keep for life.

I love her with everything I am.

Which is why last night, I decided I was going to turn down OU and follow her to New York. Something my parents did not take well. They think I am throwing my career away for a high school fling. I am not even sure I will get to continue to play for NYU for sure. But nothing matters to me more than Maddie does.

Why can they not see how much I love her?

I am deep in my thoughts when I smell strong perfume. Man, I am so glad my girl does not soak herself in the stuff. She always smells like fresh lavender and honey. It is the best smell in the world, unlike this stench. I look up and of course it is Kate, I should have known by the smell.

"Hi Lucas, all alone the day after prom? Must not have gotten a happy ending from the prude."

Who does this girl think she is? She puts on some daisy duke want to be shorts and a crop top and thinks she is the hottest thing to walk on earth.

"What do you want Kate? I am waiting for my girl, you remember her? She was prom queen." Watching her seethe and grind her teeth at the reminder that she lost prom queen to Maddie is priceless.

It is so easy to ruffle her feathers.

"When are you going to stop wasting time on her when you know we belong together?" she seethes.

This girl really doesn't know when to stop does she?

"Kate, we will never be together, I don't know how many times I need to tell you this before it sticks. I love Maddie. She is my forever." We have had this conversation more times than I can count, maybe this will be the one that sticks since I am basically yelling.

"I heard you are leaving town today. How do you think miss priss is going to manage that?" she states with satisfaction.

Why can she not just leave already? "She will manage it with me. Because we are a team and that is how we do things. Can you go now?" I respond drily.

Why is she bending down? Oh shit!!!

"Not before I get my goodbye kiss."

Bam, I am pretty sure I just threw up in my mouth as her lips connect with mine. Before I can even push her away, she is standing straight again with a triumphant grin.

"Oh look, Maddie is here. Now you can tell her about our affair and finally end it with her," she says loudly with a smirk.

She can't be serious; Maddie will never believe this garbage.

I turn around to look at Maddie with a smile, until I realize she is crying and rush to my feet. Suddenly she yells out, "HOW COULD YOU DO THIS TO ME!" and turns to run away, taking my heart with her. I jump to my feet to rush after her, and yell for her to stop, but she is in her car and speeding away before I can reach her. Fuck, this cannot be happening. I was here to tell her I choose her in every way and that stupid bitch, Kate, ruined everything in a matter of seconds. I need to get to Maddie's and explain everything.

CHAPTER SIX

(MADDIE)

I make it to my car in a flash and force this little civic to do work as I push the pedal to the floor.

I can't stop the tears that are flowing like a never-ending faucet down my face. How did this happen? How could we have seemed so happy and him to be with her on the side?

I would never have believed it had I not seen it with my own eyes. I don't think anything has ever hurt as much as this does. I don't even know how I am driving right now. I can hardly see. Let's just hope I make it home in one piece.

He is just like my father after-all. Just this morning, I was beating myself up for being negative and doubting we could do this long distance. Looks like my gut was trying to tell me something instead. I should have known that a girl like me does not end up with a guy like him. How could I be so stupid?

I can feel my heart shattering. Like, I can literally feel each piece of my heart break and turn to dust. It physically hurts to breathe. I heard him scream for me. I know he is following me. But once I am home, I will never open that door again.

I rush inside to find my mom in the living room reading. "Mom, Lucas is following me, do not open the door. I need a new phone number, like right now. Please help me" I say with desperation.

My mom looks up at my tear-streaked face and jumps up with urgency. "Maddie, what the hell is going on?" she asks urgently.

"HE IS CHEATING ON ME WITH KATE," I all but scream.

My mom looks more shocked than I feel. After a second, the shock seems to fade and is replaced with anger. She locks the door moments before Lucas is banging on it yelling for me to come out.

"Maddie, go upstairs. I will manage this," she says reassuringly.

As I make my way to my room, I barely make it inside the door before I hit the floor and sobs are the only sounds, I can hear. I should listen to their exchange, but I cannot bring myself to move.

CHAPTER SEVEN

(LUCAS)

"MADDIE, OPEN THE DAMN DOOR!!!" I shout.

The look of pain on her face is going to be engrained in my mind forever. I need to see her right now, which is why I am on the verge of breaking down the door knowing full and well her mom is likely hearing every word I am saying. Kate is such a conniving bitch.

The door opens. "Maddie, you have to listen..." I pause, because it not Maddie. It's Miss Wilson.

"Lucas, she does not want to see or speak to you. Frankly, I have watched you grow up and love you like my own son, but right now, I don't want to see or listen to you either. Get on the road. You wouldn't want to keep OU waiting," she sneers.

She doesn't even give me a chance to respond before the door is slammed in my face and the lock clicks in place.

Several hours pass and I sit in their driveway until the sun sets. I got the automated tone telling me the number has been disconnected around lunch time for Maddie and her mom. I am staring at my phone realizing she has blocked me on all social media, and I am out of options to get through to her. I need to go knock on the door again. I am about to get out when there is a tap at my window.

My dad is here? What the hell?

"Son, Ms. Wilson called me. It is time to leave and time for you to let go. I called OU and they still want you, but you need to leave now," he says as a matter of fact. As if my whole world isn't crashing down right now and I would just leave? Is he crazy? They really don't get my love for Maddie at all.

How can he expect me to just leave? I just don't get it. Did he hear nothing I said today? I love her. I turned down OU for her.

"Dad, we have been over this, I am not going to go. I love Maddie and she is my life. Football chances will come again and if they don't, they can't replace her anyways," I say exasperated with him.

After a deep sigh, my dad says, "I have already told them you are on the way and faxed the contract you signed before you changed your mind. They now own you son. You have to go, and you have to leave now, or your career is over," he states with such finality. "If you don't show up at this point, they can sue you. The signed contract is in their hands."

My dad and I have never been close.

He has never understood me. I am just the son he is trying to live out his dreams through. Now he never will.

In this moment, I know he and I are forever done. I reach into my backpack and write Maddie a letter and pour my entire heart and soul into it. I hand it to my dad, but I don't let go.

"Please make sure she gets this. Give it to her personally," I plead with him to understand the importance. "Do not let me down on this, Dad. Or I am no longer your son."

He shakes his head, clearly not amused by my determination.

"Fine son, now get on the road. We will be up next weekend with the rest of your things and to help you get settled," he says with an air of triumph and hands me a bag I did not even notice he had. I guess they packed for me and I don't even get to go home for my things. Wonderful.

Does he not realize what he has done?

"No, Dad. I don't need you for anything in my life. Ship my stuff and stay the hell out of my life from this day forward."

With that I raise the window and drive away leaving my heart with Maddie and myself hallow. I don't know how all of this happened, but I won't recover if she doesn't call me soon.

All I can do now is hope and pray she calls.

CHAPTER EIGHT

(MADDIE)
3 weeks later

Two blue lines stare back at me.

The last three weeks have been hell. My heart is in a million pieces.

I can't eat, sleep, or focus on anything and Kate keeps bragging about her visiting Lucas and how in love they are.

My mom came up after she slammed the door on Lucas's face, and tried to comfort me, but it didn't help much. I know she loves me and is here for me and after all she has been through know that I need time. I also know she ended up having to call his dad to get him to finally leave. She helped me change my number and block him on social media and has checked on my daily and been on top of me when I am home. I know I am worrying her.

Graduation is tomorrow. I leave for New York in two weeks. I scored an internship with Glamour Magazine. And... I am pregnant.

How does this even happen? I had sex one time. I am on birth control. The man broke my heart beyond repair, and I am still trying to pick myself up off the floor and now I am pregnant with his baby? His dad told my mom he left for OU, but otherwise anything I have heard has been from bitchface, I mean Kate. I am not going to tell my mom or anyone in this town about the pregnancy. I refuse to be the talk of the town. And I am not ruining my mom's joy, especially with her so proud of me graduating tomorrow with honors.

If I know one thing, I know life is sick and twisted.

I also know that I can do this. I can go to college, have this baby, and the career of my dreams. I can do it all and I can do it on my own, just like my mom did with me. She never let the pain my father left her in dictate her future and neither will I. He was a dick when I was born and not in the picture until I was almost six and left her in shambles a second time. History will not repeat itself.

Lucas will never know about this child.

I vowed to never speak to him again. He left us just like my father did and fell into some other girl's vagina before he had the curtesy to end things with me. JUST LIKE MY FATHER.

I owe him nothing.

I just need to go to sleep and focus on graduation tomorrow. The rest I will figure out after that. This will not be my nightmare. It will be my new beginning.

My mom has always said I am her greatest blessing, and this baby will be mine too. I refuse to let this pain own me anymore.

The old Maddie is dead. The new Maddie was born the second I saw those two blue lines. Tomorrow I will wake up a new person. Leaving all the pain in the past.

So, if I am starting tomorrow, I guess it is okay to cry myself to sleep one more time... I can be strong tomorrow, tonight I am going to let the pain consume me whole.

I wake up with what feels like a hangover from hell, but really, it is just from crying to long and hard. I get ready and head to graduation. My mom is coming later since I have to be there so early. Today should be a blast... not.

I almost miss them calling my name I am so in a daze.

"Finally, our final graduate of the day, Madison Wilson."

My turn to walk the stage I guess and leave this hell behind. As I make my way across shaking hands and smiling for pictures I feel no joy, but because we all know my mom is taking millions of pictures and jumping up and down while screaming my name, I do my best to make it look believable that I am excited and happy.

That's it.

I am no longer in high school. I have graduated, third in my class, with honors, and am off to NYU to leave this place behind me forever.

"Maddie, you did it!!!" My mom is beaming with pride when we are released to find our families. She is all smiles today, and maybe some tears of joy are thrown in there too.

"Mom, I am so glad it is over. Let's get out of here. I just need to go and grab my stuff from inside." I tell her. If she smiles any bigger her face is going to crack in half. Good thing I won't be telling her about the baby today. She wouldn't be smiling then.

"Okay honey, I will go pull the car around front to meet you and we can go to dinner to celebrate! We can come back for your car after. Your choice of restaurant!" She says excitedly before she walks away to get the car and I head inside to get my things.

I am almost to the room where they had us put our belongings when I hear Kate's voice in the hallway.

"Yeah guys, he said he wanted to get married. How exciting is that. But I mean, we are expecting a baby now, and it is the right thing to do. I knew I would get him all along."

Just when I thought my heart could not break any more than it has, her words cut straight through me. I walk into the room and reach down to grab my things. Leave it to Kate to not be able to avoid a moment to turn the knife.

"Oh Maddie, I hope you didn't just hear! No wait, I hope you did. I told you he was always mine. You were merely a place holder for him. We even had a bet going to see how long before he stole your virginity. Look, I even captured a photo of you in the act. I won the bet of course. I knew you would drag it out" she says arrogantly going on and on.

I don't know what comes over me, but I slap her.

Hard.

Right across the face.

"You can have him, Kate. I could not be more done with him," I scream. What an end to high school. I walk out and head for the car before anyone can respond. I try my hardest to hold my tears in.

I should have no tears left to shed. It's time to leave this all behind and be the woman my mom raised me to be.

Goodbye Boyd High School.

Wish I could say it's been fun.

CHAPTER 9

(MADDIE)

6 years later

Living on the upper east side in New York City is hectic at times, but so lively. I am enjoying the view of Central Park from my apartments bedroom window when I hear little footsteps heading my way. I am still in awe that we can now afford this place instead of a shoebox apartment. Life has not been easy, especially with New York prices.

"Mommy, look I got myself dressed today and brushed my teeth and everything," she exclaims with excitement.

She is wearing pink fuzzy slippers, little mermaid socks, hot pink shorts, and a leopard tee shirt. I cannot help but smile at my beautiful daughter. She has Lucas's clear blue eyes and his dark silky hair, with my smile and his tan skin. She is also challenged in the height department much like me, but it is our fun joke that we are fun size. I cannot believe she is already starting kindergarten today. Time is going by way too fast. I need it to slow down just a little and her to not grow up too quickly.

"Caydence, you are so beautiful. Do you not want to wear the special outfit we bought you last week?" I ask trying not to put down her choices in fashion, but also steer her in the right direction. If this is really what she wants to look like on her first day, who am I to stand in her way.

In the past, I never cared about fashion, but something about being in New York, being successful, and surrounded by fashion icons has brought that side of me to light, which is a delight for my mother. She has and always will be a diva and love fashion more than anyone I know.

"Mommy, I forgot!!!" she squeals rushing off to change. I can't help the giggle that escapes me. That girl is so full of personality and watching her run, which has a bounce to its step and looks like she is bouncing up and down with each step in that hilarious outfit is too hard to hold in my laughter.

Whew, I thought our first day pictures were going to be unforgettable and not in a good way. I make my way to the bathroom to finish getting ready for work. I decide on a black pencil skirt that accentuates my slender curves, a white blouse made of satin and my new Louis Vuitton black pumps. There is nothing better than a pair of red bottom heels. I can hear my mother's sigh of agreement in my head and laugh again.

I tend to leave my hair down in waves, but today have styled it half up with the waves coming down my back. I went all out on my eye make-up and even did a wing with some gold glitter on my lids to make it pop. I am just finishing with my mauve lipstick when Caydence dashes in dressed and ready.

"Oh baby, you look so pretty in your Lisa Frank first day of school dress. I love your sparkly tennis shoes too. What do you say? I can fix your hair like mine today?" I ask with a smile.

"YES!!! But it has to be the exact same or we will have to start all over." she says so seriously I almost laugh again with delight while she begins climbing onto my counter, something she will not let me help with. Miss independent. She has done this done since she could walk and never lets me help.

I get her hair done and check her teeth to ensure she brushed well and let her have a spray of my lavender honey perfume before we make our way to the kitchen for breakfast.

I have tried many perfumes, but nothing beats this one if you ask me.

"Eggs sound okay sweetie?" I ask while pulling eggs out of the refrigerator along with her chocolate milk and mentally doing a checklist in my mind to ensure I haven't forgotten anything.

"Don't forget the bacon, Mommy!" she says while getting situated on a bar stool.

"Of course not, only the best of breakfasts for my kindergartener!" I say with cheer.

I look over and notice she is not smiling anymore and seems upset. "What's the matter?" I ask with concern.

"Mommy, what if nobody likes me?" she says with a sad expression. This is so not like her. She is normally all sunshine and rainbows.

"Sweetheart, you are the sweetest girl I have ever known. You are going to do amazing." I say reassuring her. I am not sure if that is going to be enough but am ready to encourage her as long as it takes, even if we are late.

"You're the best, Mommy!" she says with a smile. It is moments like these that my heart seems to swell in my chest. She has such faith in me, and I am so glad she trusts my word.

Being a single parent through college was not easy. Not that being a successful sports journalist has been much easier, but somehow, it just works out the way we need it to.

I pack her lunch while she eats her breakfast and get my work bag together.

Once everything is secure in our bags, I clear her dishes, clean up the kitchen and we are heading out the door to her first day of kindergarten.

As we walk down the street, we hold hands and sing songs from The Little Mermaid, her favorite movie. She smiles at people on the street and does not have a care in the world. Everyone on the busy sidewalks of New York can hear and see her sing and sway as she goes, but it does not deter her in the slightest. She gets louder at their attention instead of embarrassed. Now that is more like my child.

She has always been so brave like that. She is so much like her father, Lucas.

Shit. Stop right there, I think to myself. You are not allowed to think about him. Keep to your rules and you will not be miserable. If you don't think about him, he can't cause you pain. It has been six years, but the pain has not lessoned at all. I still love him. But I shouldn't. I need to fix my mind before Caydence picks up on the fact that I am upset.

Who am I kidding? I will always be broken because of him, but I can at least hide that fact from Caydence.

We get to the school and head to her classroom. We were able to meet the teacher last week and see her classroom, so know exactly where to go.

Her teacher's name is Mrs. Wilks, and she seems to be very sweet. She is a middle-aged woman with short blonde hair and is short like we are. She has kind mannerisms and seems like a great first teacher for my Caydence. I am more nervous than Caydence is at this point though. How is it already time for school? We get to the classroom, and she walks in and puts her bag in her cubby with her name on it, as she was shown at meet the teacher. She comes over and hugs me.

"Mommy, you can go now. I love you," she says and kisses my cheek and runs back to her desk. That's all I get and all of her fear from earlier is gone, and she is excited to be here.

I do not know what I expected, but I should have known my independent girl would be fine. She is already talking away to the girl next to her. I turn to go, and a tear falls down my cheek. My little girl is getting so big. The teacher see's my silent tears and nods her head in understanding as I make my way out the door.

I do not know what I would have done if my mom had not moved to New York just before Caydence was born. She can work remotely and kept her from birth until pre-k as a full-time nanny, while working full time. I drop her off and my mom picks her up since I work later in the day. My mom is a saint. She took the news of my pregnancy in stride. I did end up telling her before I left for New York. I am so thankful we have her here with us.

Caydence has always been so fearless and can make friends anywhere, much like her father.

There I go again, breaking my rules and thinking about him. I am just emotional with her starting kindergarten, which must be why this is happening so much more today. I can't let this take over my emotions or I will not get a thing done at work.

With that last thought, my phone rings. It is my boss, Travis Edwards.

"Good morning, Travis! I am on my way into the office now." I say politely.

Travis can be really high strung at times, but when you work in sports journalism, having the story first is a must.

"MADDIE, GET HERE FAST! The giants just traded their quarterback for none other than Lucas Andrews!!!" he is screaming through the line.

Just the mention of his name has me frozen in place in the middle of a busy New York sidewalk and people are running me over. I have to move over to the side so I can breathe for a second.

Of course, I knew he made it to the NFL and had been playing for the Dallas Cowboys. He is one of the best quarterback's currently in the NFL. I just never thought he would end up here of all places much less with my boss calling me to give to the oh so good news.

"Maddie, Maddie, are you there?" Travis sounds anxious, not that he knows of my past with Lucas.

"Yes sir, I will be right in." is all I can manage to say.

"Good, I want you on this story. Get Becca and head to MetLife Stadium right away. He is due to arrive by midday and I need you to interview him and get photos. We have to have the story first and you are my strongest and most talented reporter. I know you can get this done."

And with that the line goes dead and my world crumbles at my feet.

I do not know how I am going to do this, but I know it's something I have to do if I want to keep my job much less be any closer to that promotion, I have been kicking my ass for.

I have worked hard to become one of the best reporters in sports journalism and rise in the ranks in the industry. There is a stigma that this a roll for men and I have to fight against it every day and if I can't do this story because of emotional reasons, I could lose my job. My boss may love me, but our company has a reputation, and I am sure he has already informed them I am the reporter coming and it would show weakness if I did not show up.

Turning down a story like this would set me back years of challenging work. But how in the hell am I going to face him? I have kept a daughter from him for six years.

But he does not know that, and never has to find out.

CHAPTER 10

(LUCAS)

My flight is due to land in an hour.

I cannot believe I am moving to New York City. When I graduated from OU, I was picked up by the Dallas Cowboys and have played for them for the last two years, but the New York Giants just traded three of their best players to have me. Not that I blame them. I am not conceited at all, but I know I am good at what I do, and a strong quarterback can make a team.

I thought I was safe from being traded, especially with my injury last season, and let my ego get the better of me. I did not think the Cowboys would let me go, but here I am. I am not mad, but I am surprised they still wanted me with my injury in play.

Honestly, I am excited for the change. It gets me further away from my father. Six years later and he and I still do not speak, but that does not stop him from trying to control my career, image and me by proxy.

When I was eighteen and he forced me into OU, our relationship never recovered. I am thankful I went; how could I not be? It got me to the NFL, but I lost the love of my life, Maddie Wilson. And that is just not something I can forgive him for.

I have not dated since losing her. I know she must think I abandoned her. I found the letter I wrote her in my father's study a month ago. So, I know he never gave it to her and that just fuels my desire to be away from him.

I should have known he would not give it to her, which means she still thinks I cheated with Kate, who ended up being pregnant with some guy from another school. Poor bastard got stuck with her for life. I do not envy him. She is not someone I would want around forever. From what I know, she is still the same nasty person. She peaked in high school and never went to college and lays around on his dime. Like I said, poor bastard.

With that shuddering thought, I wonder if Maddie is still in New York. Just as I am about to pull out my laptop and do some digging into her whereabouts, my manager comes and sits down beside me.

"Are you ready for the press?" She asks hesitantly.

She knows I hate the press and having to be in the spotlight. Why can I not play ball and still live a normal life? With this trade, my name is about to be everywhere, even more so than it was, making things even more unbearable. I hate being in the spotlight but love the game.

"No, Victoria. I am not. Why can I not get settled in and explore a bit? Do we really need to go straight to MetLife Stadium for interviews?"

Even I can hear the annoyance in my voice. I just want to settle in, maybe even find Maddie if she is even still in New York.

"Lucas, we have talked about this. After your head injury last year, it is so important to show up strong and let the world know that Lucas Andrews is still a machine." She says with sincerity.

I know she is right. I almost lost my career when I was tackled, and my helmet flew off as I hit the ground last year. I was in the hospital for months, thankfully it was the last game of the season, but I cannot help ending that train of thought and bring my focus back to Maddie.

Not even a brain bleed could get her off my mind. I will never stop loving her. I even tried to get in touch with her mom over the years so I could get in touch with her through her, but she has always given me brief updates, like she is doing great, wonderful career and bullshit things I love to hear, but won't give me her contact information or address and says if she wanted to find me, she would. So many people believed we were a high school fling, but they have no idea how much more we were, but that's when a thought hits me.

"Fine, but if I do this for you, can you help me with something?" I ask with determination.

"It is not for me. It is for you." She rolls her eyes. I know I put her through hell. "What do you need help with?" She asks looking skeptical.

"I want you to find out if Maddie, or Madison Wilson is her full name, is still in New York. She went to NYU for journalism, and I need to find her. She went to Boyd High School with me back in Texas" I state firmly with a new determination to get my girl back.

"Do you mean Madison Wilson, sports journalist?" she asks as if she knows her.

"I am not sure what type of journalism she focusses on." I state with curiosity. Could Maddie be working in sports and know I made it? Maybe I have a chance to find her, and a chance is all I need to keep hope alive.

"Well, if it is the same girl, watch out. She is a shark and always finds her story and right now, you need only positive press. No one needs to know how bad your injury was" she says flatly before getting up to go back to her seat.

She turns around one more time and pauses. "Do you know her date of birth?"

I give it to her and smile knowing she will find her for me even though she doesn't want to.

And with that I head back to my seat with a determination I have never felt about anything. I will make Maddie mine again if it is the last thing I do.

CHAPTER 11

(MADDIE)

As I enter the office and hit the elevator button for the top floor to Bleachers Report, it dawns on me that this is the first time I have dreaded going to work. I know the moment I walk into my office; Travis will storm through the door with Becca closely behind him and we will begin discussing the interview with Lucas.

It is not that this is not wonderful for the Giants or something, but my history with him that is making me sweat.

I have not laid eyes on him since I saw him with Kate six years ago, but I look into his eyes every time I look at my daughter and that is hard enough and I love her with all my heart.

He cannot find out about Caydence. Of that I am certain.

It is a long train ride to New Jersey and since we are meeting with him at MetLife Stadium, I know we have to leave rather quickly once I arrive since he gets in at midday, yet I find myself picking the elevator with the most people on it, knowing it will be more stops on the way to the top.

As we climb the thirty floors slowly, stopping on almost every other floor, I cannot help but reflect on my time with Lucas.

I was so in love with him. I haven't dated anyone in the past six years, but I cannot say that is fully due to him having my heart.

I am a single parent after all. I clawed my way through three degrees and have been working full time since the day, I saw those two blue lines appear.

We finally hit my floor and the second the doors open; Travis is on my heels and speaking a million miles a minute.

So much for making it all the way to my office. I am barely making out a word he says, he is speaking so quickly, until he states, "I secured you a private meeting with him before he meets with everyone else and he has requested you meet with him alone, so Becca will be out in the main lobby with everyone else and you can join her when you are done. She can make sure you two have front row seats for his Q&A."

IS HE CRAZY!

I can feel my heart beating rapidly and am about to respond when my phone rings. It is not a number a recognize, but I know I need to answer it to give myself a moment to pull myself together.

"Hello?" I say in my professional tone.

"Hi, my name is Victoria, and I am Lucas Andrews manager," she says plainly.

"Hello Victoria how may I help you?" I know my tone is dryer than it needs to be, she has done nothing wrong, but she works for the man who shattered me to pieces so that it all it takes for me to be frosty.

"I have reserved conference room B for you and Mr. Andrews to meet in at noon. I have been instructed to reiterate that this meeting will be between you and him alone. Your assistant may not attend the meeting." I can hear the distaste in her tone. She doesn't like this anymore than I do.

"Will you be joining us in the meeting, Victoria? I ask with a tiny ray of hope.

"No, Mr. Andrews has requested to manage this meeting on his own against my insistence he should not do so. I will meet you in the lobby and escort you to the conference room and your assistant can wait in the lobby with the rest of the reporters." She says with a disgusted tone. Well, at least I am not the only one who thinks this is a bad idea. Maybe I can convince her she needs to remain in the room.

"Victoria if you would be more comfortable attending the meeting, I have no qualms with that." I say as a last-ditch effort to get out of being alone with Lucas.

"Yes, that would be my preference, but Mr. Andrews has insisted he do this alone." She says in a defeated tone. "If you do not have any other questions, I will see you at noon." She says more professionally this time.

"No, Victoria. No questions. I will see you at noon," and with that the line goes dead.

Why does he insist on being alone with me? Does he know it is me he will be meeting with, or does he just want a chance to leak his story his own way and without interference?

It is no secret he had an injury last season, but it is my understanding that he is perfectly fine now. My thoughts are cut short when Travis begins speaking.

"Maddie, this meeting could be your chance to make editor, which would double your salary and set you up for success. I do not need to stress the importance of this right?" He asks with hesitation.

"No sir, I have everything under control. Are there any specific things you would like me to dig into that may not be on my list?" I ask, switching to my professional mask I have so strongly put into place. This career is cutthroat, and you have to have solid masks to survive. Never show weakness.

"No, I trust you have everything under control." He says with admiration in his tone and all hesitation gone.

My mask must be very firmly in place, which is good since I am heading into the lion's den and he seems confident in me again.

"How was the first day of kindergarten?" He asks out of nowhere. I am surprised he remembered, but probably only because I put it on his calendar, in red, that I would be late today.

Becca makes her way into my office before I can respond. Did she dress up for this? She normally has on these awful pink glasses and dresses in boxy styled clothes, but today she has on a red bodycon dress that hugs her in all the right places, contacts, and black stilettos.

As if she read my mind she says "Travis, do I really need to dress like a barbie for this interview?" Now I can see how uncomfortable she is. Her tone is anything, but happy.

"Yes, he has a type, and we want him to notice you and answer your questions first and foremost. He has only been spotted with a woman a couple of times, but they all look like this" Travis is annoyed again and rolling his eyes.

He is not far off though. With her hair down her back in waves and her make up overdone, and with the too tight dress and heels, she is doing an impressive Kate right now.

Dumb bitch...

"I don't think she needs to dress in a way that makes her uncomfortable to get the job done, Travis." I state realizing I am jealous and that is dangerous territory.

He has a baby with Kate, what am I even doing? And how has that not been leaked to the press yet? Clearly, they are not still together or that would be all over the media. At least there is that.

"She will stay in that and you two need to head out. You look stunning as always which is why you did not receive instructions on how to dress. Do you have your recording devices, cameras, and notebooks?" He says brushing me off as if I had not spoken.

Typical Travis...

"Yes, we have everything. Let's head out Becca." I say so dryly even I am surprised and taken back. Letting my professional mask slip is not something I do, but no one seems to notice, and Becca and I head for the exit.

We get on the elevator and are both quiet. "Are you okay, Becca?" I ask concerned because she is normally very talkative.

"I am not comfortable in this crazy outfit. I cannot believe Travis is making me wear it. Since when do I have to change how I dress to get the job done?" She says exasperated.

I feel for her.

"Do you want to swing by your place and change? We can stop again on the way back and let you change back?" I ask knowing she will be more comfortable and this jealous streak I have going will be much happier.

"YES! I was scared to ask." She says with relief in her tone.

"You never have to be scared with me." I say reassuringly.

Before I know it she is all changed into a boxy pant suit, and we are on the train.

Becca is reviewing facts and statistics about Lucas and trying to find any information she can on his injury, and I am staring out the window.

Normally, I would be preparing as well, but when it comes to Lucas, I have stayed informed even though I always told myself not to.

There is nothing she could research that I do not already know. My nerves are at an all-time high and somehow, part of me is excited to see him.

I will never let that show and will have my professional mask in place when we arrive, but for this moment, I am letting myself be lost in my thoughts.

CHAPTER 12

(LUCAS)

Our private plane just landed, and I could not be more excited to see Maddie. I am not even nervous. I will finally be able to tell her the truth about Kate and with us in the same city, I may have a chance to get her back.

I just hope she likes who I have become. Victoria always calls me an alpha male, but something about being so close to seeing Maddie has me feeling soft and using manners again.

I must admit, my heart stayed with her and in turn, I have been quite the asshole over the last six years without it.

I do not have many friends, or anyone I am truly close to. I have my teammates, but I stay surface level with them. I keep everyone at arm's length because I do not have anything to give anyone else while my heart is nonexistent without Maddie.

I have more money than I know what to do with, but that does nothing to make me happy. There is no happiness without her.

"Lucas, I am having your driver take your bags to the penthouse after he drops us off at MetLife Stadium, and all your other belongings have been delivered to your penthouse suite. Your cars are in the garage. We reserved the top floor of it as you asked." Victoria is going on and on about things I do not care about, but I should be a lot more grateful for.

"Victoria, did you complete all the details for my meeting with Maddie? I know I just cut her off and sound like a dick, but right now I do not care.

"Yes, Lucas. I am meeting her in the lobby at noon and bringing her to you in conference room B. The only conference room with no windows as requested." She says with an eye roll.

"I am sorry I have been such an ass." I say, even shocking myself.

"Lucas, I have been with you for the last two years. I am used to you and yes you are an ass." She says with amusement.

I cannot help but chuckle, as I am pretty sure she is the only one who can successfully put up with me.

"I know this meeting makes you nervous, but can I tell you something personal?"

"Lucas, I do not know if there is much, I don't know about you at this point." She chuckles.

"Have you ever seen me with a woman?" I ask with a smirk, because yes, there are still things she does not know about me, and it will almost be fun to shock her.

"Are you about to tell me you are gay? Oh man, or worse yet, you better not be in love with me, because I hate to break it to you, but my husband would be pissed considering we just moved to New York for you. But to answer your question, no I haven't beyond the dates I have set up for you as needed." She says with amusement.

She is such a smart ass, but it is why I keep her around. She can put up with my shit and still be witty and not a total bore to be around because it does get lonely at times.

"No, I am not gay smartass. I am in love with Maddie Wilson. I have been since I was a kid." I say with a smile.

Her mouth is literally hanging open. There is not a witty response or any attitude in sight. I may have broken her.

"I know, I know. It is a shock. She is why you never see me with women. I lost her when this bitch we went to high school with convinced everyone she was pregnant with my baby and I was cheating on Maddie and then my dad sent me off to OU against my will using a contract I had signed, but not sent and I never got to even explain myself to her." Sadness has entered my voice and my head hangs low. That is as much detail as I can get out without being a major asshat and crying or some shit.

I have missed Maddie so much.

"I do not even know what to say. I am honestly shocked, but I have to say as your manager, I really think you should make this a professional meeting and arrange another time to speak to her. You know her boss assigned her this case and by not coming back with a story, she could very well lose her job and have even more reason not to hear you out. She is a success in a field run by men. This could break her and push you two further away" Becca says seriously.

The look of worry on her face and the way her voice wavered as she spoke tells me how nervous she was to say the words, but she is right, I do not want to do anything to push her further away.

"I will conduct a professional interview for her, but when that voice recorder goes off, I am going to say what I need to say, because you are right, I do not want to push her away."

That's when it hits me.

"I am going to talk about my injury and give her the story I have refused to give anyone else." I say with determination knowing Victoria is about to start yelling.

"YOU CANNOT DO THAT!!! We have worked so hard to keep everything under wraps for your career, Lucas!" she says with more anger than I have ever seen from her.

"Listen, we have about an hour until she gets there. Can we meet in that conference room together and brainstorm about what I can release without jeopardizing everything you have worked so hard to protect? I want to give her what no one else has and make her boss happy, and maybe then she will agree to meet with me outside of work and I can finally get my girl back ya feel me?" I say and I know I am begging at this point.

"Fine, we can discuss what you can and CANNOT say. But I am only agreeing to this, because you are my friend and employer and I have love for you and want you to get your happy ending, but I hope you know I need a bonus or some shit, because I am about to have a lot of work on my hands along with unpacking, because not all of us have people to do that for us and are coming home to a decorated and unpacked pent house." She kept a stern tone, but at the end she broke into a smile.

That's when I knew for certain, she has my back in this and is going to help me get my girl. "Victoria, I will pay for someone to come take care of all of that for you and give you a ten-thousand-dollar bonus on top of that if I get my girl." I give my signature smirk that does nothing for my happily married manager and bounce in me seat with excitement. Maddie, I am finally coming for you.

CHAPTER 13

(MADDIE)

That train ride went by way too quickly. We are crossing the street and then we will be at MetLife Stadium.

We are a good thirty minutes early, just the way I like it. I thought I would be nervous, but I have firmly put my professional mask in place and am ready to get to work.

I want to ask his manager a few questions before I meet with him. Since she will not be there, I want to do my part to make her feel comfortable with the private meeting.

I know if it were me, I would be worried about details slipping that I did not want released to the public, and though I would love the story, I do not want to cause her stress or leak something that would truly hurt his career, because it is Lucas after all.

"Maddie, are you ready for your private interview? I am so jealous! He is so hot." Becca says with a dreamy expression.

"I am." I say flatly. I hate that she thinks he is hot. I am glad she changed and looks more normal and less sexy right now. I know, I am insane. The last thing I need is for him to notice her and them start dating. That thought makes me nauseous.

"Are you sure? You have been short and quiet the whole way here." She asks with concern.

"I am fine." I say confidently.

"If you are not up for it, I can do the interview and you can wait to get your questions in with everyone else?" She says kindly not knowing it makes my blood boil.

I know she is asking to be kind to me, but it still frustrates me, which only makes me more upset, because Becca is my friend.

"No, I have this under control, but thank you for thinking of me." I say as kindly as I can considering I am about two second away from poking one of her eyes out. I know she is a good friend and has no idea why this would upset me, but still, it makes me see red.

"I wish I was only thinking of you, that would be way more honorable than dreaming about getting him alone." She laughs.

"BECCA! What kind of shit is that to say? Be a professional, would you?" At this point she is flat pissing me off, but again, she is my friend, does not know about our history and I need to calm down.

"Yes ma'am, sorry ma'am." She says and hides her face from me.

"Becca, listen, that came out harsh, but this story is a big deal and I need you to get your head in the game. Both our careers depend on it right now. If I get this promotion, so do you, we are a team." I say the words, and I mean them, but deep down, I know I also do not want her to hit on him and that bothers me more than I care to admit.

We enter the building in silence. I know I have likely hurt her feelings, and I need to apologize better, but this is not the place.

No one is in the lobby yet, which is good, it gives us time to go over our notes and maybe I can get my apology in after all.

"Look, I am sorry I bit your head off. I am really wanting this to go well." I say sincerely.

"It is okay. You are right, I need to get my head in the game here and not act like a 24-year-old for a second." She says with a smile.

We start pouring over notes together and decide what questions are most prominent. The fact that the question "are you gay?" is on the list is hilarious to me, but I keep it to myself.

A pretty woman in a navy pant suit walks in and I assume she is Victoria and stand. She is way too pretty for my liking. Blonde long sleek straight hair, a fitted pant suit that shows off her very slim curves, about five inches taller than my short five foot build and she has the new Gucci heels I would die for. Great, so this is what he is used to being around. I look horrible next to her. She makes her way over and introduces herself.

"Hi, I am Victoria, we spoke on the phone." She says with a smile.

"Hi Victoria, I am Maddie, and this is Becca, my assistant and partner." I say happily bac

"Partner huh? You are a different breed, I do not know many who would give her assistant so much credit, props to you for recognizing her that way. Nice to meet you Becca." She says kindly.

"Oh, she deserves the praise, I assure you. I would be lost without her." I say proudly before Becca can even respond.

"May I meet with your briefly before I meet with Lucas, ugh, Mr. Andrews." I cannot believe I just said that. I could kick myself.

"Of course, and honestly, he prefers Lucas and hates all the fuss." She says politely, which makes me feel slightly better.

"Becca, I will be back, stay here so you ensure a front row spot as the other reporters arrive." I say and pat her on the back.

"You got it!" She smiles.

With that, I follow Victoria to the conference room, and she stops right outside the door and faces me.

"I wanted to speak with you before the interview, because I know it cannot be easy for you to not be in the room. Is there anything you want me to avoid asking him? I want you to be comfortable with us meeting." I am back into professional mode, just in time too.

I need to have my head on straight to make it through this.

"He wants to give you the exclusive on his injury. Is there any chance you would be willing to let me proof that information before you publish it? This is already going to cause me a hell of a lot of work, and it would help me prepare by knowing what I am going to be dealing with ahead of time." She says with a polite smile, meanwhile I am so shocked that I forget to breathe.

"Why me? He has not talked about this with anyone." I am so confused.

"He said it had to be you. It will get out eventually and he wants you to be the one to write it." She says and I see something in her face that makes me wonder if she knows he and I have history, but I am not opening that can of worms.

This is business and if she does not know, I would look beyond unprofessional.

"I am flattered. And yes, I will let you proof my article before I publish it, but please do not tell my boss." I say with a chuckle.

"I have to know, are you always this accommodating or is this a first? I have heard you are very cutthroat." Did she just say that with a straight face?

She is very to the point, isn't she?

"I am indeed cutthroat. This is not something I normally do, no, which is why I would like my boss to be none the wiser." I say seriously.

"I see why he chose you." She says with a smile.

And with that, she leaves me to enter the conference room.

I take a moment to breathe and prepare myself. I am about to see the only man who has ever owned me, mind, body, and soul.

Oh, and don't forget he still holds my heart.

Here goes nothing. Time to knock.

CHAPTER 14

(LUCAS)

I am strangely calm for a man about to see his girl for the first time in years. I do not care what anyone says, she is still mine.

I had Victoria do a quick search and she found that she is not married. Now, I can only hope she isn't seeing anyone.

I hear voices outside the door but cannot make out what they are saying. Good, that means this room is close to soundproof and we will have privacy.

It's been quiet for a minute or two. Maybe it was not her outside of the room after all.

Just when I am about to text Victoria to see what is taking so long, there is a knock at the door.

I stand to open the door and realize that it may be better to stay seated, so I am not so close to her and do not immediately try to wrap her in my arms.

"Come in." I say with authority in my tone and way louder than I normally would, but clearly the room is close to soundproof since I could not hear them.

She opens the door and holy shit.

She is even more gorgeous than I remember. And man, that tight black skirt she is rocking is sexy as hell. Her white blouse has just enough cleavage to be classy but smoking hot. And oh, my lord, are those fuck me heels?

Shit, I have to get my mind under control, or I am going to have bigger problems that are hard to hide in gray slacks.

"Hello Mr. Andrews." She says formally extending her hand to shake, which I respond to in kind and firmly.

59

"Hello Maddie." I say with a smirk. "Thank you for agreeing to meet with me. I wanted to give an exclusive that I will not be sharing with the media after this meeting." I say with a smile.

Get it together, get it together, get it together. Be the alpha male here.

"I appreciate the opportunity to publish your exclusive." She is being completely professional. Fuck.

I kick myself; I need to do the same for the time being.

"May I record our meeting?", she asks while taking out a voice recorder.

"Yes, of course you can." I say warmly. Professional Andrews, you can do this.

"Okay, thank you. It is on now. I have a list of questions I would like to ask you, but you stated you have an exclusive for me, would you like to dive into that first or for me to ask my questions?" She is pulling out a notebook and pen and has yet to truly make eye contact with me.

I have my work cut out for me.

"We can proceed however you would like." I say smirking again. Not that she can see since she refuses to look up at me.

"Okay, let's get my questions out of the way." She finally looks up and I swear my heart skips a beat. I cannot hold back my smile.

"Ask away, Miss Wilson." I say still smiling.

"I know this is crazy, but no one has spotted you with a woman in the two years you have been in the NFL, so everyone is wondering, are you gay?" I can't believe she just said that with a straight face. I am dying trying to hold in my laughter.

We lost our virginity to one another for fucks sake. She knows I am not gay.

"No, I am not gay, but I gather you know that already." Whoops. So much for professional, but who was I kidding, I am an athlete, not a businessperson.

I chuckle at myself.

"Something you find funny, Mr. Andrews?" She asks trying to hide a smile. Oh, how I have missed her smile.

"Not at all." I can't help the smirk that is playing on my features.

"How do you feel about your trade to the Giants? You were not with the Cowboys very long but were very successful in your first two years." She asks looking down and taking notes, I guess on the gay thing. I cannot help the chuckle escapes at that.

"I am excited for this change. I loved playing for the Cowboys and will miss my teammates but am eager to meet the new team and begin training." I say more professionally, maybe I can be professional to an extent.

"I have more questions, but I want to leave some for my assistant and the others out there and am eager to know what you want to tell me about your injury." She says with an eagerness, and for the first time, I see how much she loves her job, and it brings me joy too.

"How did you know it was about my injury?" I ask because I did not mention that was what it was about.

"I spoke to Victoria about it and assured her I would not make her life difficult." She says matter of fact like. She is sexy as a professional, but I miss my Maddie.

"Ah, I see." I rub my chin for a moment and try to recall everything Victoria discussed with me before this meeting.

"As you know, I had a head injury at the end of last season. My helmet even came off and I hit the ground without protection." I pause to let her take her notes.

She is so beautiful. Her hair is longer than I remember.

"I was taken to the hospital. It was not a minor concussion as everyone thinks. I had a major brain bleed and had to undergo brain surgery so they could repair the bleed." She looks up at me with concern all over her face.

"They did what they could to repair it, but there is still damage, meaning, I have to be extra careful not to repeat the injury, otherwise it could be the end of my career." I hope I am making the right decision in releasing this information.

"I see why you have not released this information. It could make coaches hesitant to want you. Are you sure you should still be playing?" She asks and I cannot help but notice how scared she looks.

A sign she still cares. Bingo. This is my in, fuck this interview. Somehow, I manage to answer her question with those thoughts running through my mind.

"Football is my life. If I could not play, I would have nothing, because I lost the woman I love around six years ago." As soon as I say the words, I know there is no going back. Guess I couldn't hold it together after all.

She picks up the recorder and drops it into my glass of water I had on the table.

"I cannot do this story. It could ruin you, Lucas." It is the first time she has said my name informally and it sends a jolt through me.

"Maddie, I wanted you to write the story, because I trust you to take care of me. It will eventually get out, and I want you to be the one to do it." Before I know what, I am doing, I am reaching across the table and holding onto her hand.

She is staring at our intertwined hands deep in thought.

"Maddie, I never slept with Kate. I never betrayed you. She was pregnant with some other guy, and they are now married and hating life. She saw you and set the whole thing up. I left you a letter, my dad refused to give it to you. It is in his study to this day, not that I talk to him anymore. Maddie, you have got believe me, I never stopped loving you. My father forced my hand with OU. He sent a signed contract in and I would have never played again had I not gone and could have been sued. I told my parents I was turning down OU to stay with you and that is what I wanted to tell you the morning you say Kate force a kiss on me and run her mouth. I had been telling her to leave me alone. You have to believe me."

I spit it all out, in one breath, and now I have to wait for her response, and I have never been more scared in my life.

CHAPTER 15

(MADDIE)

I am struggling to process everything he just said.

Did I hear him right?

He is still holding my hand and it is like an electric shock, but in such a good way. Did his eyes get bluer? I am in a tailspin, and I do not know what to say or do right now.

I look at my watch, we have twenty minutes left of our set time. I need to say something, it has been almost two minutes of silence, but I am reeling at everything he said.

He did not cheat on me.

Could it really be true?

"Maddie, please talk to me. I swear on my life I am telling you the truth and I am still in love with you." He sounds like he is pleading with me, but that could be my imagination, because his tone carries an authority now that I am not accustomed to.

"Lucas, how can this be? I thought... it doesn't matter what I thought. All these years, I have been in so much pain. I loved you with everything in me."

Shit, I just said that in past tense, and he looks like he is in pain.

"Loved?" One word is all he said, but I can feel his anguish, because I love him too.

Without thinking, I stand and walk around to his side of the table, straddle him, and slam my lips to his with urgency.

His lips are even softer than I remember, and he immediately wraps his arms around my waist and kisses me back like his life depends on it.

I can feel him hardening beneath me. He moves a hand into my hair and deepens the kiss by tilting my head and then I feel his tongue begging to be let in. I open right away and our tongues dance together like they were always meant to.

A soft moan escapes me, and I press myself into him further.

 Maddie, I have missed you so much," He whispers has he works his way down my neck.

Without thinking, I grab his tie and start undoing it.

He grabs it and just when I think he is going to toss it, he grabs my wrists and ties them securely behind my back.

I know my panties are drenched and he has to feel that even through his pants. But this side of him is all new to me and nothing like the sweet time we had before.

He stands and I wrap my legs around him and I have to trust him to hold on to me as my arms are tied behind my back.

He plants me on my feet and turns me around to bend me over across the conference room table. The cool surface feels amazing because my skin is on fire.

He is kissing my neck from behind and holding on to my hip while the other hand works its way up my skirt.

Moans are falling like prayers from my lips at this point. He is the only man I have ever been with, and it was nothing like this.

"Maddie, spread your legs for me now." He demands with an authority that shoots right to my core. I do as he asks, and his hands find their way to my soaking wet panties.

"So wet for me, Maddie, so ready." He says in almost a growl.

He instantly shoves my panties to the side and his thumb is on my clit stroking and rubbing and suddenly two fingers enter me without warning.

I come undone on the spot and moan his name repeatedly and loudly.

An orgasm hits me like a car slamming into a brick wall without warning and I can barely breathe. He doesn't stop his torturous rhythm until my body relaxes and slumps further into the table.

"I am just getting started, sweetheart. I am never letting you go again." And those are the last words I hear before there is a knock at the door.

"GO AWAY" he screams out.

"Lucas, it is time for the press conference, are you two almost done?" Oh my god, its Victoria. I stand instantly.

"Untie me right now." I demand. He does so quickly in case someone comes in.

I fix myself as quickly as I can and rush over to my purse to get my mirror and make up. I put myself back together in a flash when he is suddenly in my ear behind me.

"This is not over. Come to my place tonight."

Shit. I have Caydence. What the hell am I going to say here. I cannot tell him I kept a daughter from him all these years, because of a lie a bitch told.

What have I done? And how am I going to fix this or make anything work with something like this looming over our heads?

CHAPTER 16

(LUCAS)

Blue balls suck.

But watching Maddie come undone like that was pure bliss. Why isn't she saying anything?

"Lucas, I cannot come tonight, I have other obligations." Here we go all formal again. This is not the girl that just came and straddled me a second ago.

"Maddie, don't you believe me?" I ask panicking.

"Yes, I honestly do believe you, but I truly cannot come tonight. I need to plan in advance and make sure I have a... I just have to plan in advance, okay?" She is hiding something from me, but now is not the time to push her.

"Okay, Maddie, it's okay. Just promise me that I can see you again." I say calmly and sweetly.

I will not let her go again.

"I promise." She speaks.

"Shit, I did not get anything for a story. I just blew my chance at my promotion and not just mine, but Becca's too."

I have no clue who Becca is, but the look of defeat on her face is enough to break me.

"I will have Victoria email you my story. I will make sure you have everything you need, but I just want one thing in return. Okay, two things." I say with certainty.

"Thank you so much," she throws her arms around me and hugs me tightly.

Why do I have this press conference, I just want to leave with her.

"Condition one, you publish my story, I know you said you want to protect me, but I need this to get out the right way." I pause.

"Condition two, you give me your phone number." I say and my smirk is back in place.

"Deal," she says with a smile.

I lean down and kiss her one more time.

"I will see you out there, please tell Victoria I need a moment. I need to get my dick under control before cameras start flashing and get my tie back in place." I say while laughing.

"I am so sorry to leave you like this." She says sadly.

"Hey, listen to me. Trust me when I say that getting you off like that was the best moment of my life. You have nothing to be sorry for." I say and put my fingers in my mouth to taste her and it's so damn good.

She is blushing and I can see the hunger I feel in myself reflected at me through her eyes.

Then she grabs my fingers I had just had in my mouth and puts them in hers and sucks on them with a soft moan.

Good lord, I am going to bust right here in my pants. Get it together Andrews.

"See you out there," she smiles over her shoulder as she leaves the conference room.

As soon as I am alone, I know I am forever hers. She owns me, and I could not be happier about that.

When I finally emerge from the conference room, Victoria is smirking at me in that way I know all too well.

"Have a good meeting in there stud?" she can't even hide her laughter.

Ignoring her comment, "Listen, I need you to email her my story. Get her card before she leaves and send her everything we discussed." I say with that arrogance she knows me for while trying to get past her question.

"What, you did not have time to get it out with all the sex you just had?" She is such a smartass.

"You smell like sex, Lucas. Go clean up, it's time to face the beasts." She laughs and walks away.

"Just get it sent to her!!!" I yell back on my way to the bathroom.

"Already done boss, somehow I saw this coming." She smirks and then is gone around the corner.

I head into the bathroom to get cleaned up when my phone pings.

I pull it from my pocket to read the message. **"You asked for my number, so here it is. Victoria was kind enough to give me yours. Now get out here before they start rioting hot shot."**

I save her number and reply.

"When can I see you again."

I hit send and head out to my version of hell.

My phone goes off again.

"Tonight, I am free after all."

YES, that is what I like to hear.

I send her my address and put my phone away and head into the press conference feeling lighter than air.

CHAPTER 17

(MADDIE)

I cannot believe my mom called and asked if she could keep Caydence tonight.

She heard about Lucas coming to town and called to see if I was alright. When I told her I was the one having to interview him today and see him, she said I needed a night to myself.

I told her what he told me as quickly as I could, and she insisted I go this evening.

I told her I wanted to pick Caydence up from school and take her to get ice cream and hear about her first day and then she could pick her up and I could get ready to see Lucas. She was shocked to hear I would be seeing him again but did not protest. She had tried to tell me that Kate's baby was not his years ago, but I would not hear it so she probably assumes I now know and want to tell him about Caydence.

My mind is anywhere, but on the press conference when I hear my name.

"I have decided not to give much away today. I am providing an exclusive to Ms. Madison Wilson with Bleachers Report. I will take minimal questions but be prepared to hear no comment for many of my answers." He is so confident and calm. Normally, people get at least a little flustered with the press, but not Lucas.

I cannot believe he just said that.

These reporters are going to go ballistic on him. And just as the thought crosses my mind, everyone starts speaking at once.

"Mr. Andrews, why the exclusive?"

"Mr. Andrews, I can do a better exclusive than her!"

"Mr. Andrews, please don't do this, we all deserve a shot."

"Mr. Andrews, what makes her so special."

Victoria suddenly quiets the room so he can speak.

"I chose Ms. Wilson, because I believe her to be the most talented journalist in this room. I believe she will write the truth and not smear my name in the process, and she has my trust."

Again, the room goes wild. I feel a hand on my shoulder and Becca is right beside me.

"We should get out of here before this gets any crazier." She looks kind of panicked and I realize she is probably right.

He does realize this is being televised right? He just handed me the keys to his story, and I know without a doubt, I will do right by him, I owe him that much with what I am hiding.

As soon as we cross the street and are in a safe zone, Becca turns on me.

"What the hell did you say to him to get this exclusive? Travis is going to worship the ground you walk on!" she asks eagerly.

I have no idea how to respond, because it is not like I want to tell her what happened in the conference room.

"I have no idea, but I have my work cut out for me." As soon as I finish my sentence, my phone is ringing, Travis...

"GREAT WORK WILSON! I don't know what you said in your private interview, but I look forward to reading your notes and first drafts of this article. You just put yourself on the map kid." He says with excitement.

"Thank you, Travis. I am meeting with him this evening in his personal residence. I would like the rest of the day off to prepare." I say hoping he will respond well.

"You got it kid. Take as much time as you need. Tell Becca she can have today off as well. Job well done ladies. You just nailed the promotion for the two of you." And with that he ends the call and I let out a squeal.

"WE GOT THE PROMOTION!!!!" I shout with excitement.

"And we get the rest of the day off!!!" Becca and I are literally jumping around in the street!

"I don't know how you did it, but damn girl, I am so proud of you!!!"
She exclaims proudly.

"Thank you, Becca! I could not have done anything without you, I
hope you know that. You deserve this promotion as much as I do." I say
and instantly hug her.

"I am going to go enjoy this day off and prepare to hit the ground
running with you tomorrow, but you should come get that insanely
hot red dress Travis bought me for your meeting tonight." She says
excitedly.

"You know what? I think I will." And with that we head to her place so
I can pick up the dress.

With the dress in hand, I head to pick up Caydence from school. I
cannot wait to hear all about her first day. I get there in record time and
when she comes out of the school to the pickup line, I am so happy to
see her smiling.

"How was your first day sweetie?" I ask her with a smile.

"Mommy, it was the best day ever. I love my new big girl school!!!" She
says while giggling and smiling.

"How about some ice cream to celebrate?" as if I don't know the answer
to that question.

"YES!!!!!!!!!!!" she screams.

With that we head off to Coldstone Creamery and she tells me all
about her day. She talks about recess the most of course, but then,
suddenly she seems sad.

"Mommy, why does everyone else have a mommy and a daddy and I
don't? Didn't my daddy want to be here today too?" she says and then
her lip pouts out as if she is going to cry.

I don't think I have ever felt more awful. I kept her and Lucas apart all
these years and for what?

He did not even cheat on me in the end and we spent all these years
apart when he could have been here watching his daughter grow and
now she is sitting here asking about him and sad.

All my previous excitement vanishes as I realize I am going to have to tell him the truth and he is going to hate me forever and I will lose him all over again and Caydence will never get to know the wonderful man that is her father, or worse, he could try to take her from me and he would have a good chance at winning that battle considering I hid her for the last five years she has been alive.

Not to mention, I am going to let Becca down, because when all this comes out, I can kiss my promotion goodbye, which means she will as well.

Worse, I could lose my job for not letting them know I was not the person for this job, since I had a personal relationship with the client and that is what is going to cost us the story.

"Baby, your daddy is a wonderful man, and it isn't his fault he isn't here. You are too young for me to explain, but I promise I am going to try to fix everything so he can be in your life okay? I want you to know that if he isn't and mommy can't fix this that it is in no way your fault, but all mine," I say sadly.

"Mommy, no matter what happens, I will always love you and think you are the best mommy." She says and hugs me tightly.

Little does she know; I have made a huge mess of things and may not ever be able to put things back together.

What have I done?

CHAPTER 18

(LUCAS)

Well, this press conference has gone to shit.

Everyone is losing their mind, demanding I answer some questions and screaming.

"If everyone could please quiet down, I have a statement," Victoria says as loudly as she can.

The room goes quiet, except for the sounds of clicking cameras.

"Mr. Andrews has decided to do an exclusive piece. You are all going to have to except that, but I will say that he is very excited to be here and joining the Giants. He enjoyed his time with the Cowboys but is eager to meet his new team and begin training with them. We hope you all have a great day and thank you for coming out to welcome him here."

Man, this woman is a pro, I need to get her that bonus she said she needed for this.

We make our way to exit and to the town car she had arranged. Once inside the car, I take a much-needed breath.

"Thank you for stepping in back there and for having my back with this decision." I say with sincerity.

"I think it is a great idea and we can spin the story our way with Maddie. Plus, it is going to be fun watching you try to get the girl." She says with a chuckle.

"She agreed to come to my place this evening. She said she has some things to take care of and then she will head over." I say with a smile, something she normally does not see on my face.

"Would you like me present? Do you still want me to send over your story to her or will you be going over things this evening? I already sent a highlight reel as I told you earlier, but I was planning to send her a full write up to her personal email that covers more than the notes she didn't get to take because you were all over her." Something about the smirk on her face has me thinking she knows that is not what I want to spend my evening doing with her and it is obvious she knows my interview with her was less than professional at this point.

"Listen here, smartass, I can get work done too, but I don't feel like proving this point, so you can send over the story." I say with my signature smirk in place.

"I thought you might say that, which is why I drafted the story during your "meeting" and it is already waiting for her in her inbox along with the highlight notes I sent while you were "interviewed" Which she highlights with air quotes. This woman..."You guys can discuss what I sent and make any changes, which I would like to see before it goes to her boss." She says with a knowing grin.

"Then you can go on with whatever plans you have for her this evening." She laughs, "and I don't need the details on that part."

"Thank you, Victoria, for everything. This really does mean the world to me. How does a fifteen-thousand-dollar bonus sound? I know this is going to create a lot of work for you." I say seriously "So, it seems like it is worth more than the ten I said earlier."

"That sounds great." She smiles.

The driver drops me off at my new penthouse, which I have not even laid eyes on yet and I tell Victoria to use the car to get home.

Nice building on the upper east side. I hope I am not too far from where Maddie lives. I make my way into the elevator and swipe my special key card that allows me to go to the top floor.

When the space opens, I am shocked. Victoria has not only had everything delivered, unpacked, and decorated, but the place looks amazing.

Black leather couch, sleek modern furnishings throughout the house. A modern kitchen is stocked and even has groceries already. The master bedroom has a four-poster bed in a dark wood and has a masculine feel, while still being comfortable.

There are three guest bedrooms which are decorated and done well, along with a study I will never use. Not too shabby if I do say so myself. I shoot off a quick text to Victoria thanking her and a text to Maddie with my address since the original text did not send and then head for the shower.

When I get out, I check my phone and notice Maddie and Victoria have texted me back.

"No problem bossman" is Victoria's reply.

I switch over to Maddie's messages already smiling.

"Wow, you are in my building. What a coincidence."

Wow, I am in her building. Victoria needs a raise on top of her bonus for this one even though she did not even know about Maddie when she picked this place.

"What time do you think you will be here?" I say in a quick message to Maddie.

I put my phone down and decide I should dress in jeans and a polo, giving a more comfortable vibe. I style my hair in the messy style I tend to rock, shave my face again so it is perfectly smooth and opt for my polo sneakers to finish it off. I apply cologne and decide to explore the house some more.

I am making my way to the kitchen to see what kind of supplies I have so I can decide if I want to cook for her or order in when I hear my phone go off.

"I can be there in about an hour."

She replies. Sweet, I think I will order in.

"What sounds good for dinner? I am going to order in. Feel free to come casual and be comfortable."

I add on so she knows she can be comfortable.

"But I have this sexy red dress that is just dying to be worn. There is a pizza place called Marcos on 5th, they have the best pizza."

Red dress? Now I have to see this.

"Red dress huh? I think I need to see this. I will order the pizza. Want the usual?"

Her reply comes in quickly.

"I am surprised you remember, but yes, pepperoni and pineapple please!"

Some things never change.

I go online and get the pizza's ordered and decide to walk down the street and get us some wine and beer. Since I have no idea what she likes in that regard, I opt for a sweet white, and two different reds. I snag my coronas and make my way back. When I get into the elevator, I see Maddie's mom, but she has a little girl with her.

I wonder whose kid that is?

"Ms. Wilson, how nice to see you again, and who do we have here?" I ask with a smile.

"My name is Caydence and I like to sing Little Mermaid songs." How cute is she with her sweet voice and blue eyes?

"Lucas, hello. We were just leaving. I will catch up with you another time. Caydence come on sweetie." She grabs Caydence's little hand and hurries off, but then I hear it...

"Okay, Nana."

What the hell? Maddie is an only child and if this kid is calling her Nana... Holy shit, Maddie has a kid.

With my mind still reeling, I make my way back upstairs knowing Maddie will be here soon, but that little girl is all I can think about. I love kids and I am fine with Maddie having one, and judging by our actions this afternoon, the father is not involved with Maddie.

I hope he is at least in his kid's life. I am lost in my thoughts when my phone rings. "Sir, we have a Ms. Wilson down here asking to be let up?" the front desk says. "Yes, please send her up." And with that I hang up, she is here, and I have questions.

CHAPTER 19

(MADDIE)

When my mom called and said she and Caydence ran into Lucas in the lobby, my heart sank.

I thought I would have some time with him before I had to tell him the truth. I am still not sure what I am going to say to him.

How do I go about saying, oh by the way you have a daughter who is five years old?

When you left six years ago, I was pregnant and never told you. There is no way he missed the resemblance; she looks so much like him.

I make the way up to the top floor in the red bodycon dress, some silver Manalo pumps and my Gucci purse.

I may look amazing with my hair down in waves the way he likes it and some amazingly done make-up, but I know I am visibly shaking.

The doors open into this beautiful modern penthouse.

I am in awe of how gorgeous this is. And I thought I did well? HA! He is standing there looking quite dashing if I do say so myself. That polo hugs him in all the right places and his jeans fit like a glove.

"Maddie, you look breathtaking. I am glad you did not come casual and decided to wear that." He says with a smile.

Maybe he didn't make the connection between him and Caydence after all?

"Thank you, you look quite dashing yourself." I smile.

"Pizza will be here any minute. Do you want to eat in the dining room or here in the living room like we used to?" He asks.

"Living room sounds great." I say and know it came out shaky.

"Maddie, you have a daughter." Welp, there it is, he is jumping right into it.

"Yes, I do." I say looking at the floor.

"Hey, look at me" he says and now, he is right in front of me with his hands on my shoulders.

"That's okay. I love kids. She is gorgeous just like you." He says with a warm smile.

So, he did not make the connection.

"Thank you, she is my world." I say honestly. Well, as honest as I am brave enough to be right now.

"What happened to her father?" Well, shit...

"He is not in her life. Well, honestly, he does not know about her." I say with a half-truth. Why can I not just tell him?

"I am so sorry, Maddie. I am here for you alright?" He says so earnestly, my guilt begins to swallow me hole.

"Thank you," I say in nothing more than a whisper.

I get a slight reprieve when the front desk calls to let us know the pizza delivery has arrived.

We sit down to eat, and he has provided wine, which I take a glass of white thankfully. I need some liquid courage right about now.

"Victoria sent you over the story, do you have any questions we need to go over?" He asks since I have been sitting silently for a good ten minutes.

"No, she outlined things amazingly. Thank you so much for this exclusive. My boss is over the moon. I will draft up the article tomorrow in the office and send it over for you and Victoria to review." It feels good to talk about work and not the elephant in the room.

"Great, I know you will do the story justice." He says proudly.

We finish eating while watching Friends reruns and move to sit more closely together on the couch. I just want to feel him, smell him, and enjoy hum for a little while before I have to drop the bomb that he has a kid. Maybe that makes me selfish, but I have missed him for over six years, and I just need him for at least a little while before he hates me.

I need to tell him, I really do. And when I turn to do just that, deciding my selfish desires are not important, his lips meet mine instead.

What starts out as a gentle caress quickly builds to more, but how can I do this when I have something so heavily on my mind.

"Lucas, stop. I need to tell you something." I say while looking at my hands.

"I am sorry, I have just been dreaming about this moment with you over the last six years. There has been no one since you and I know that isn't the case for you, which hurts, but I am okay with it. You are single now though, right?" he is speaking quickly.

It's now or never...

"Lucas, I have not been with anyone since you either." I say the words and wait for them to sink in for him.

His eyes go wide, and he looks dumbfounded.

"Maddie, we have never lied to one another. You have a daughter. Clearly, you have been with someone else." He says defensively.

I know this is the moment where everything will change and I may lose him, but I know he is a good man, and even if he hates me, maybe he won't take my daughter from me and will love her anyways.

"Lucas, Caydence is your daughter." I say pensively.

I swear his face has just turned white as a ghost. He gets up and begins pacing the room and I have no idea where this is going to go, but I have never been so afraid in my life. He still has not said anything almost ten minutes later.

Should I leave and give him time to process the bomb I just dropped on him?

Should I stay and beg him to understand?

Will he ever understand?

I was eighteen years old, I thought he had gotten Kate pregnant, and he left for OU.

I was young, what else was I supposed to do besides raise her and keep moving forward with life?

Will he understand?

I should have told him. I should have called him.

What if he can never forgive me?

"Lucas, I am so sorry. I am going to go and give you time to process this information." And with that he turns to look at me and it is the iciest expression I have ever seen.

In this moment, I know I have lost him forever, and the pain that sears through me is worse than when I saw him with Kate all those years ago.

CHAPTER 20

(LUCAS)

Did she seriously just say Caydence is my child and then plan to walk out of here like she did not just change my life forever.

I am in utter shock and disbelief.

I have a daughter.

That would make her what? Five or six years old? Shit, I have missed five years of her life? And she thinks she is leaving right now?

"You are not leaving." I say in a demanding tone, which causes her to wince and move further away from me.

"Lucas, I just wanted to give you some time to process. I am sorry, I was not trying to upset you more." She states like this is nothing.

"Maddie, how old is she?" I ask and can hear the anger in my own voice.

"She is five. She started kindergarten today." She says while looking at her hands.

"How could you have kept this from me for five years Maddie?" I ask in disbelief.

"I thought you were having a baby with Kate and had been cheating on me. You left for OU and your father said you never wanted to see me again. I thought about calling you, I really did, but part of me thought it would only make things more painful and I was so broken after you left. I ended up in the hospital twice before I even left for New York and nearly lost Caydence. I knew telling you could make everything so much worse, and I was afraid, okay? I was only eighteen years old and had to learn how to be a mother and was hurting after losing you. I made a mistake, and I am so very sorry." When she finishes, I see tears have started streaming down her face.

I may be mad at her, but I still love her, so I move closer and wipe her tears with my thumbs and hold her.

"Maddie, I did not cheat on you. Do you hear me? I didn't do it. Kate is just a bitch and wanted to hurt you after you not only got the guy but made prom queen. You have to believe me when I say that I have never and would never cheat on you." I take a breath to get my anger under control.

"I am livid that I have missed five years of my daughter's life, and livid I have missed this time with you, and I swear I am trying to understand here, but I am upset and need some time to cool off. Maddie, I love you, but please just give me a moment. And my father did what? I leave him a note explaining my side of things and he goes and does this instead. I am sorry, but that makes me even more angry than your confession, because had he given you the note, I might not have missed out on my daughter." I say and lift her chin to look at me.

"I love you, Maddie."

With tears flooding her face at this point, she replies, "I love you so much. I am so very sorry." She isn't just crying, she is sobbing. I try with everything I have to cool my anger and succeed so that it is merely a simmer. I don't want to scare her.

So, I pull her into me and hold her instead to give myself a little more time and having her close helps me cool down.

"I am not willing to lose any more time with her. I want her in my life and to meet her right away." I say seriously once I know I can do so in a calm, but serious tone.

"Lucas, please give me the time to tell her about you. She is only five and she won't understand why I haven't told her about you yet. My relationship with her is everything to me. I know I messed up, but please let me talk to her first. I know she is going to want to meet you too. She has asked about you many times." She says still laying her head on my chest. Her tears are soaking my shirt and as upset as I am, I hate to see her crying or in pain.

"What have you told her about me?" I ask while trying not to dwell on her tears, because I know I will give her anything to make them stop and I don't want to wait to meet my daughter.

"She doesn't know about Kate and all the reasons around why, because she is only five, but I told her that you did not know about her, and I would find you someday and tell you." She says with hesitation.

"So, she doesn't think I abandoned her?" I ask in shock.

"No, of course not." She says and sounds taken back.

"Thank you." I say quietly.

"What are you thanking me for. I just dropped a bomb on you and hid a daughter for the last five years." She says sadly.

"For not making her hate me before she even knows me." I say honestly.

"I know you want to talk to her first, but I want to meet her tonight. Now if possible. I want to be there for her too. You are not alone in this anymore, Maddie." I say sincerely.

She hesitates to respond for a minute or two.

"Okay, Lucas. I will call my mom and have her bring her home. We can head down to my place and talk to her together. But please be patient with her and me. I have done this alone her whole life and it is not going to come naturally to depend on someone else." She says with defeat in her voice.

This is it, the moment I am going to meet my daughter.

I wanted Maddie back, but now will gain a daughter too. And I have never been more determined than I am now to make us a family. That's how it should have always been, and I am not going to miss out on any more time with my girls.

I give her a moment to make the call and when her mom agrees to bring her home after they finish dinner, I spend this time asking as many questions as I can about her.

CHAPTER 21

(MADDIE)

"What else do you want to know about her before meeting her?" I ask with a grin.

He has asked me about all her favorite things, color, music, movie, things to do, hobbies, and so much more. He went from shocked to wanting to know everything about her in seconds.

"When will you two move in with me?" he asks seriously.

"Woah, Lucas. I have not seen you in six years, she does not even know you yet, I have no idea if you and I work together as adults. How can you even ask me something like this?" I say feeling defeated.

So much for the happiness we were jumping into together.

How could he think that we could jump right into living together and being a family?

"Okay, I will wait." He says but seems to have something else on his mind.

"What are the chances of you agreeing to marry me then?" He has his signature smirk on his face, so I know he is serious right now.

What is he thinking? It has been six years. We have not dated since we were children ourselves.

"Lucas, what are you even talking about? We have not even gone on a date. We do not know each other as adults." I say the words because someone has to be responsible here.

"Maddie, you are it for me. I have known that since I was a kid. I have no doubt in my mind that we are meant to be together, but if you want to date and take things slowly, I can do that for you, but I want to be a part of Caydence's life and not lose any more time than I already have." He says confidently.

"Lucas, I know you are eager, sure, and confident, but I need time. I would like to introduce you as my friend this evening. Spend some time letting her get comfortable with you and spend some time getting to know one another again before we jump in headfirst." I know this is what I need for us to do.

I have raised her on my own for her entire life and we need to get to know one another again and not just uproot her whole life.

"I will work with you, Maddie and do everything I can to make you comfortable, but you have to let your guard down and let me in again." He says pensively.

Does he not understand how much it hurt to lose him the first time and how hard it was to build myself up to where I am now?

He says he will work with me, and all I can do is hope for patience and that this will work. Either way, he knows about Caydence now, and no matter what, he is going to want to be in her life.

"Are you going to take me to court?" This is my biggest fear.

"No, as long as you do not try to keep me from her life, I see no reason why we cannot work through this together, that said, I owe you five years of child support, so if you would like to go to court, we can." He says while looking me straight in the eyes.

I can see it in his eyes. He is willing to do whatever it takes to make this work. He is putting the ball in my court.

"You do not owe me anything. I should have told you about her from the start." I say and I know he can see the shame written all over my face.

"Maddie, you did what you felt was best given the circumstances as you knew them. Please do not beat yourself up over things you cannot change. I was mad for like two seconds and then realized that myself and do not blame you for the choices you made. I called my father while you were arranging for Caydence to come home and he admitted to what he did and that he knew about Caydence. If anyone is the blame, I blame him and I blame Kate." He says with venom and then jumped right to another questions about Caydence. "Where does she go to school?" He asks.

"She attends St. Jude School for Girls." I answer hesitantly. "Why?"

"It is not that uncommon for a father to want to know where his child attends school. Relax, Maddie. I mean no harm, but I would like to pay her tuition for the year." He says with his smirk in place.

"Lucas, that tuition is very high. She is on scholarship currently, but that may change with you in her life and being as wealthy as you are." I say with sadness. He can offer her so much more than I can.

"Hey, money doesn't mean happiness, baby. It is nothing without those you love to share it with. I have lived a very lonely existence. I would have rather struggled alongside you and not know wealth." I know he said that to make me feel better, but instead it angers me.

"Excuse me, I do very well for myself. Have we struggled along the way? Yes, but I am a very successful journalist and have done a damn good job of providing for the two of us." I scream back at him.

"Maddie, I meant no disrespect. I was just pointing out that having funds does not mean life was sunshine and rainbows for me." He is using his placating voice, so I know I am being sensitive.

I keep saying how it has been six years, but I still know him very well, and clearly, he knows me too.

"I am sorry. I am nervous is all." I say quietly.

"Do you think she will be more comfortable in your apartment, or would you like to tell your mom to make her way up here?" He asks, and all I can think about is how he is already putting her comfort first and my heart is swelling in my chest because of it..

"My place. She will likely want to show you everything she owns and tell you a million stories." I say with a smile. I love my baby girl.

"When do you think your mom will get here with her?" He asks suddenly looking nervous.

"An hour maybe? Why?" I ask wondering if he is going to back out and changed his mind, but without warning he has shifted on top of me on the couch, forcing me to lye back and grabbed my hands and has them pinned above my head. His lips come crashing down on mine and all my stress floats away.

CHAPTER 22

(LUCAS)

It feels so good to have her firmly trapped beneath me. All I have done is secure her arms and kiss her and she is already moaning. I let go of her hands, but only long enough to pull my belt off. I know we need this moment of intimacy together after so many emotions have come in in just a short period of time.

"Maddie, give me your wrists." I say as a demand, and she complies right away.

I use my belt to secure her hands and lift them back over her head. "Do not move your arms, do you understand?" I say firmly.

"Yes sir." She says with a sultry look on her face. I begin to kiss her again, this time demanding her to open up for me so our tongues can dance.

I use her neck to tilt her head forcing her to deepen the kiss which earns me another moan.

I let my other hand tug on her dress and force the neckline down.

Hell yes, no bra, once I have her breasts free, I begin to tweak her nipples. I spend a little time on one and then the other and continue to switch between the two enjoying her moaning into my mouth. I release her lips and work my way down her neck, careful not to mark her, but also rough enough to make her squirm beneath me.

I finally make my way to her right breast and suck it into my mouth and use my other hand to continue my torturously slow pace on both at the same time. She is bucking beneath me, but my weight holds her in place. Suddenly her fingers are in my hair.

"Ms. Wilson, I told you not to move your arms." I say sternly.

"But Mr. Andrews, I am dying to taste you." She says in the sexiest voice I have ever heard. I sit up and she drops to her knees in front of me.

I release her hands and she goes to work on my jeans button and zipper going painfully slow since her hands are tied. No doubt payback for my slow teasing earlier too.

She finally frees my cock and strokes it slowly before licking the precum off the tip. Before I know it, she has licked my shaft to tip and moaned the entire time.

Suddenly, she puts it in her mouth and begins to suck. My hands make their way to her hair and grab on tightly.

With every suck, she takes me in deeper. "That's it baby, take me deeper." I say, but know if she keeps this up, I am not going to last long, but she obeys immediately, catching me by surprise as she takes me in all the way to the hilt. I can feel myself sliding down the back of her throat and let out a loud groan of pleasure. "Yes, baby, just like that."

"Maddie, oh god, stop or I am going to come." I say breathlessly, after a couple of minutes of her working me with her mouth while now using my grip on her hair to push her in faster and control her movements. Where did she learn to give head like this?

"Maddie, I can't hold on any longer," I warn and seconds later I am shooting in the very back of her throat and she is swallowing every last drop and sucking me clean.

She licks me all over and ensures every last drop is consumed before looking up at me with a smirk.

"I had to pay you back for earlier, she smiles." Oh, hell no, she thinks this is done?

I pull her dress the rest of the way down and stand her up and watch it fall to the floor. She is wearing sexy red lace panties, which leaves little to the imagination.

I grab on to the lace with my teeth and rip them off her body which results in a squeal. "I hope you weren't attached to those." I say but give her no chance to respond as I grab her and lay her out on the couch.

I spread her legs wide and stare down at her gorgeous pussy which is so wet and ready for me. Clean shaven, just the way I like it.

Without warning, I dip my head down and suck on her clit hard. She lets out a loud moan and her restrained hands find my hair instantly. "Hands above your head and do not move them unless I give you permission, princess or I will have to punish you." I say in a stern demand. I don't play around with slowness this time; I suck hard and fast and let my tongue work its magic.

"Oh god, yes sir." She screams out and puts her hands above her head where I had put them when I first restrained her.

I can see she is already close, so I reach down and plunge into her with two fingers. She bucks and thrusts into my hand and fucks my face and I don't let up for a second.

I can feel her clenching around me, so I pick up my pace, add a third finger and nibble on her clit. That does it, she is moaning uncontrollably and coming all over my face. I lick her clean, as she did for me and make my way up to kiss her deeply, making her taste herself on my lips.

Without breaking our kiss, I plunge into her entrance and begin to fuck her hard and fast. The couch has slid back a few feet, but like I care. She screams out when I go all the way to the hilt and my balls slap into her ass. I break the kiss to look into her eyes and she winces in pain, but that look quickly turns to fire and passion. I pull back only long enough to pull my polo over my head and watch as she rakes in the view. I am not a kid anymore and am packed muscle and have an eight pack, but she stares at my chest where he name is tattooed over my heart.

I continue slamming into her as she cries out my name and her nails claw their way down my back. She finally stopes looking at the tattoo and looks into my eyes. I squeeze her hips harder and trust as hard as I can twice. I hope that leaves a mark. Just as that thought hits me, I decide to leave a mark of my own and drop to her breasts and begin to suck until several marks are left behind marking her as mine. She is moaning uncontrollably and I know she is about to come.

"I am going to come" She screams out, "Oh god I am going to come, Lucas."

And feeling her clench around me is what pushes me over the edge, and we come together in total ecstasy.

I sit up because I do not want to crush her and pull her to the other side of the couch on top of me. I gently stroke her back and know that I somehow have to convince her that this is forever, and we have always been meant to be. I am never letting her go again.

"I love you, Lucas." She says barely above a whisper.

"I love you too, Maddie, more than anything."

I know we need to get ourselves put back together so I can meet Caydence, but I need to hold her for as long as time allows. I reach down and release her hands and she instantly snuggles into me and wraps her little arms around me.

"I love you too, Lucas." She says and I feel the love in each word.

CHAPTER 23

(MADDIE)

After the best moment of my life, and being cuddled up next to him, I make my way downstairs for a quick change of clothes and to freshen up.

My dress is ruined, and he ripped my panties off, which was just about the hottest thing ever, so I am currently in one of his tee shirts and nothing else. Walk of shame much? He didn't want to leave me, but he needed to freshen up as well and there is no way I was coming down here like this to greet my mother and my daughter. He is meeting me down here in fifteen minutes and my mom should be here shortly after. I take the world's fastest shower and I put on leggings and a tee shirt and make my way into the living room thankful that I cleaned yesterday, and the house is put together.

After being in his penthouse, my place looks mediocre, but nice. He knocks on the door, and I open it up wide for him.

"Wow, Maddie. This place is amazing.

He looks around at all the photographs of Caydence through the years that adorn my walls and stops at each one. He then heads into the kitchen and examines all her artwork I have pinned to the refrigerator.

"It isn't as nice as your penthouse, but I have worked hard to make this a home." I say with a smile.

"Maddie, this place is better than mine. My apartment may be big and fancy, but this is a home. Can I see the rest?" He asks with a warm expression.

"Sure." I take him on the tour.

He already saw the living room and kitchen. I show him my room next and then take him to Caydence's room which is decked out in mermaids. The tour does not take long since we live in a small two-bedroom, two-bathroom apartment, but in New York City, this is considered a ton of space.

"This place is amazing. Her room says a lot about her, but I tried not to notice too much, because I am hoping she will show me herself." He says and I can see he is excited.

We sit down on the couch and not even a minute later, Caydence bursts through the door with a huge pouty face.

"Mommy why are you ruining my sleepover with Nana???" she pleads with her bottom lip poking out.

"Caydence, I wanted you to meet my friend. His name is Lucas. Can you remember your manners and say hello?" I say sternly, but with a smile.

"I know you already. I met you downstairs." She says matter of fact.

"Ah, yes you did, but I did not know you were Maddie's sweet girl at the time, and I was dying to get to know you." He says with a warmly.

"Can I show you my toys?" She asks excitedly. How did I know this was going to be the first thing she did?

"Of course, you can, lead the way." Lucas gets up and follows her to her room. I want to follow, but I also want to give them a minute.

"Maddie, I am going to sneak back and tell her goodbye. I have a feeling he is going to want some time with her this evening. We can do our sleepover another time. Are you doing okay though?" My mom asks.

"I am. I am nervous, but I am glad this is happening. She has been asking about her dad more and more, and I think this is just what she needs. I can fill you in on everything later." I respond back as confidently as I can.

Caydence comes running back into the room with Monopoly in hand and with Lucas closely behind her.

"Mommy, Lucas said we could all play together. Isn't he great?" She squeals.

"Hey Caydence, Nana is going to head home, you have fun, okay? I will see you tomorrow after school." My mom says and hugs her goodbye before making her way out. But Caydence stops her before she opens the door.

"Nana, don't you want to play? I thought we were having a sleepover?" She gives her the best pouty face I have ever seen.

"Nana is a little tired baby. Can we have a sleepover this weekend?" My mom hits her with her megawatt smile and Caydence stands no chance.

"Okay Nana, I love you!" she runs and hugs her again before returning to set up Monopoly and my mom leaves.

After three games of Monopoly, we decide it is time for Caydence to take her bath. I go in and wash her up well and get her into pajamas and leave her to brush her hair herself like she likes to attempt to do. So far, the evening is going off perfectly. They have laughed together and teamed up to beat me in the games. I saw Lucas cheating and giving her his landmarks and money. Cheater!

Lucas is sitting on the couch deep in thought. "What's on your mind?"

"She is so much like you. I am in awe of her. You have done an amazing job raising her." He says sweetly.

"Thank you." I respond shyly.

"When are we going to tell her I am her dad?" He asks.

"YOUR MY DADDY?" Caydence says loudly.

Shit, this is not how this was supposed to go.

"Caydence, come sit down baby." She comes and sits in my lap.

"Listen, Lucas is your daddy, yes. We have not seen each other in a very long time, but he wants to get to know you and be in your life. What do you think about that?" I ask as calmly as I can, but inside I am screaming.

"I would like to get to know you, Caydence. I don't want to miss a single second with you." Lucas adds.

"Where have you been for so long?" Caydence asks him.

"Caydence, Lucas and I lost touch many years ago, and so he did not know about you. Now that he does, he wants to be here." I respond before he can.

"Caydence, if I had known, I would have been here for you." He adds and it is like a knife to the heart. It is my fault he has not been here. And now Caydence knows that too. Anger tries to find its purchase, but I don't allow it to.

"Well, if you promise to never leave again, you can stay. Are you and Mommy married?" She asks so innocently, but I sit shocked into silence not for the first time where Lucas is involved.

"I would very much like to marry your mom. Maybe you can help me convince her?" He says with his smirk in place. I could smack him right now.

"Mommy, you should marry Daddy. He is very handsome." She says sweetly. I am going to get him for this. "Mommy he has blue eyes like me!" she exclaims. "Is that why you love mine so much? Because you love his eyes mommy?"

Shocked by her question, it takes me a second to answer her. "Yes baby, I loved his eyes from the time I was a little older than you and still do now." I say and look up at him and smile.

This is all going to be okay. I just need to take this one day at a time.

"Mommy can Daddy put me to sleep tonight?" she asks.

"Yes of course he can, sweetie." I answer her and just like that our world has changed forever. It isn't easy for me to miss out on bedtime, but I know they need this time together, so instead I eavesdrop from the hall and listen as he tells her a sweet bedtime story about a little boy who fell in love with the girl next door.

I do not know how I feel though. It has been Caydence and I against the world her whole life and now I am going to have to adjust to Lucas being in the picture as well and as much as I feel for him, she is my world, and I am not sure how this is going to work.

CHAPTER 24

(LUCAS)

I did not know what to expect when meeting Caydence, but it is like my whole life now has meaning.

My heart grew inside my chest, and she is now my everything. I feel warm and almost complete, the only thing that would make it better is to convince Maddie to be mine.

Caydence asked me to put her to bed tonight and I have no idea what I am doing.

The fact that I have missed so much already, and she is walking me through a bedtime routine I should already know is heartbreaking. I am trying to be forgiving and understanding as to why Maddie kept this from me, but I cannot deny that I am hurt. I can't help but just watch on like some lunatic as Caydence brushes her teeth and asks me to help brush her hair out. This doesn't solely lie on Maddie though. I hate my father for making me miss all of this. And I hate Kate even more for what she put us through. I cannot imagine the pain of thinking I was not only cheating but had a baby with someone else while she did all of this alone.

"Mommy normally puts my hair in a braid at night, otherwise I cry in the morning when she has to brush it. Can you do a braid?" She asks so sweetly and innocently, and I feel like shit right away, because no, I do not know how to braid.

"Why don't I go get Mommy and let her do the braid?" I ask knowing I sound sad. If I had been here this whole time, maybe I would have learned.

"Mommy!!!!" Caydence yells out. "Daddy doesn't know how to braid hair, can you come help him do it?" I hate that I don't know how, but this is a chance to learn something new and hearing her call me Daddy made me forget why I was upset a second ago.

Maddie makes her way into the bathroom and shows me slowly how to braid. This is like rocket science. I am going to need a lot of practice.

"See easy!" Maddie says with a playful smile. She knows me well enough to know I am totally lost.

Now that she is all ready for bed, Maddie kisses her cheek and tweaks her nose and says she loves her before heading back out of the room.

I have her tucked in tightly like a burrito as she called it and tell her the story about a boy who loves the girl next door. A small glimpse into her mother and me.

"Now is when Mommy kisses me goodnight and turns on my night light over there and leaves, but she leaves the door cracked open, so I don't get scared." She tells me in her sweet little voice. " I really liked that story. Mommy normally reads a book, but I like your way better."

I smile and kiss her forehead and I turn on the night light and kiss her cheek one more time for good measure just like Maddie had done and tell her I love her and to have sweet dreams. I am at the door and about to walk away when she calls for me.

"Daddy, please don't leave again. I want you to stay forever now that I have you." Her voice sounds like she may be crying, but with the light off, it is hard to tell.

I kneel beside her bed and hold her little hand.

"I won't go anywhere. I promise." And it is a vow I intend to keep.

I decide to stay a while and hold her hand, but she is asleep in minutes. I make my way back to the living room to find Maddie in her pajamas. She looks so beautiful. She has never needed anything to enhance her beauty. She is already stunning.

"Did you fall asleep in there or did she talk your ear off. I was about to come cut you guys off, so she isn't tired for school tomorrow. It is already passed her bedtime." She says with a smile.

"She fell asleep almost instantly, I stayed a few minutes and watched her sleep." When did I become a sap?

"Lucas, its almost midnight. You were in there for hours." Wow, it sure felt like minutes to me.

Now I am standing here awkwardly. I told Caydence I was not going anywhere, but I did not say I was staying the night and would be here when she woke up. I hope she understands.

"Listen, I may have messed up. I told Caydence I would not leave her again, but I did not explain that I would not be here in the morning." I let out a long sigh and know I have already messed up.

"Lucas, you can stay here tonight. We can explain to her tomorrow that not all Mommies and Daddies live together and are married and sometimes they must share their time with their kids when its like that." She says quietly and I can tell she is uncomfortable.

I am not sure what to say to that. I don't want to be like that. I want to be with Maddie and Caydence every day and never miss anything else.

"Why do we have to explain that? We should be together Maddie." I know the irritation in my voice isn't something she missed.

"Lucas, listen, I do not think we should rush into anything. We haven't seen each other in years and don't know one another as adults. You have no idea how much a kid changes things." Well look at that, she mirrored my irritation. I would understand had she not hid this from me for years.

"Maddie, whose fault is that? You kept her from me, and you are not doing that ever again." I say raising my voice.

"Would you be quiet? She just met you do you really want her to wake up to yelling right now?" Her face is turning red, and I can see that I am only making things worse.

Why is she even mad right now? She is the one that put us in this spot and would not listen to me back in high school.

"You have no right to be mad at me right now. I did nothing to deserve this, no matter what you thought back then. I am trying to be understanding and forgiving here, but you are not going to fault me for wanting to be a family with the woman I love and my daughter." I say, again with my voice too loud.

"I am going to pay her school for the year tomorrow, and you are going to have to accept that. I am her father. I will not allow you to dictate what I do for her. I am also going to want to see her and you won't get in the way of that or we can solve this in court." As soon as the words leave my mouth, I know I have royally fucked up. The last thing I want to do is go to court and come in making demands.

"Excuse me? You do not get to show up and turn our life upside down or make demands of me. I am her mother, and you are stranger!!!"

Her vein on her forehead is popping and she is bright red with anger.

"Turn your life upside down?" I am about to dig this hole deeper, but my anger isn't letting me see that right now.

"You finally come back into my life, which has been a shell of what it was after you left me for something I did not even do, and then I find out I have a kid I knew nothing about, and I am the one turning your life upside down." I am so deep in this hole. I don't want to fight; I just want to be let in.

"Get out." She says with finality.

"I will tell her you had a early practice and had to go. We both need to calm down and right now I cannot even look at you. You said you would not take her from me and here you are threatening court and everything else. Get out now." She says void of any warmth and I know that she means it.

"Listen, I don't want to go to court. I should not have said that, but I want to be a part of her life. I want to be with you. I have waited so long to have you back and I do not want you to push me away." I say calmly this time.

"Maddie, I never stopped loving you and I loved her the second I laid eyes on her. Please give me a chance here."

"Fine. Stay. I am going to bed." She says and walks away without a second glance.

I knew this would be hard, but I never thought it would be this hard. I need to get over my anger fast before I blow this and lose her again.

I also do not want anything to get in the way of being with my baby girl.

She walks back out. "Here," she hands me a blanket and pillow, "sleep on the couch." She states flatly.

I decide to walk up in her personal space and throw the bedding on the couch and crash my lips to hers. She doesn't push me away, which shocks me, so I step in closer and put my hands in her hair.

When a small moan escapes her, I know I need to step back. We were already intimate, and I do not want her to think that is all I want.

With my hands still in her hair, I press my forehead to hers, "I love you; I don't want to fight, I just want to be here." I say softly.

"Lucas, I love you too, but I am terrified and do not know how to handle any this and need you to slow down." She says breathlessly.

I take her hands in mine and kiss her cheek. "I will slow down, but do not push me away. We work Maddie and need to try to learn to be a family."

With that, I let her go and she walks to her room, and I make myself comfortable on the couch. I play sports for a living and work my ass off, but that is nothing compared to the fight I am about to have to put up to keep my family.

I decide to pull out my phone and call Victoria. I need to fill her in on everything, because no one is going to care about my injury when this leaks. But I find a message waiting for me from Maddie.

I love you too.

I can't stop the smile that takes over my face. I quickly shoot a text to Victoria and roll over to go to sleep.

CHAPTER 25

(MADDIE)

Three months have gone by, and Lucas has been wonderful.

He shows up every single day. He has taken some of my mom's days and picks up Caydence from school and they go on dates, he has learned to braid her hair and knows her routines, he stays over constantly and has semi moved in, and I have fallen madly in love with him all over again. He never pushes me but is always there at the same time.

I know he wants us to be a family and he has done everything to show me just that.

Tonight, is his first game with The Giants and the news of his child and love for me has spread like wildfire, even more so than my exclusive he gave me, which not only earned me my promotion, but helped my career take off in spades.

People responded well to my story about his injury, and it got even more traction with the news of our relationship and child together. He wants us at the game, so I have let Caydence's school know she will be out tomorrow, and I have taken the day off work since we will be out late.

Things are moving quickly and though he basically already lives with us, he wants to officially move in, well, he wants us to move upstairs to his place, which makes sense because it is so much bigger, but I so appreciate that he has basically been living with us so Caydence is in her own space and comfortable.

I am on cloud nine, but I can also still feel myself holding back and I know he feels it too. I don't know what is holding me back, which makes things difficult, because it is hard to address something I do not understand.

Caydence and I just got home from shopping.

She wanted to get Giants gear with her Daddy's name on it and I decided to take her for a manicure and pedicure and make a day of it. Lucas is busy with his team today, so we had some much-needed mommy daughter time today.

I am finishing up my hair and make-up with her watching my every move.

She has a gorgeous Elsa braid with loose curls framing her face and my hair is curled and has a small braid at the top to match her. We look cute if I do say so myself.

"Mommy, would you say yes if Daddy asked you to marry him?" she blurts out of nowhere.

I take a second to think carefully about how to respond.

"Sweetie, I love your father very much and we are both here for you even if we are not married right now." I say hoping I have answered her correctly without putting ideas in her head, while also not dismissing the idea.

She doesn't need to know I am terrified to fully commit for some reason.

"I think you should marry him." She says with a certainty I wish I felt.

"Maybe someday sweetie. We should get going, because Daddy wants you to meet the team and see everything before the game." I say trying to change the subject.

We make our way to the game and like always for the last few months, cameras are flashing, and everyone wants a picture of the secret woman and daughter in his life, which is why Lucas is paying for security to follow us around when in public for a while until this dies down. I can't even get Caydence to school without someone trying to get a picture. Once inside, Lucas is there waiting and takes us and shows us the offices, locker rooms, training rooms, and even takes us out on the field.

We are standing together at the twenty-yard line when I notice our families are already in the stands and we are on the jumbotron. I am honestly shocked to see his father in the stands.

He is there with Lucas's mom, Victoria with her husband and in the row in front of them sits my mom, Becca and even Sarah, my best friend since high school.

That's when I see it, he is behind me, on one knee, and it all clicks and makes sense. Why are families are here, why when I decided to get manicures Caydence was so thrilled, why we had to match and look so cute and be here so early. It hits me like a bolt of lightning, all my fears melt away and all I want is to say yes.

"Maddie, our roads have been bumpy, and things have not always been perfect, but life is not perfect without you in it. I would rather have bumpy roads with you then ever live without you. We have the most amazing daughter and family and I want to make it complete. I love you both so much." He pulls out two ring out of the elaborate box. "I know I am never going to be perfect, but I hope I can be the perfect man for you. I love you with every fiber of my being and I have seen life without you and it is empty and worthless and I never want to know that feeling again. You two are everything to me and I don't want to live another second without making you both mine." He pulls Caydence to his knee so she can sit on it.

"Will you marry me, and Caydence, will you let me truly be your daddy every day?"

I know tears are falling down my face, and I swear my heart is bursting out of my chest. Caydence screams out her answer before I can.

"YES!" and she wraps her arms around him and squeezes tightly and when she lets go he slides a tiny diamond on her finger and now they are both looking at me. I smile and pull him to his feet. He looks terrified of my answer.

"Lucas" his face falls, he must think I am about to say no, "Yes, I want to marry you. Can you kiss me now?"

His face comes up and his smile is radiant. Our families are cheering from the stands and his lips crash onto mine. He reaches out and pulls Caydence in to join our embrace and screams, "FINALLY!"

I never saw this coming. I never thought I would get the man I have loved my whole life, such a wonderful daughter and feel as happy as I do right now.

My world is complete, and I am filled with love. I have no idea what was holding me back, but nothing will ever keep me from him again.

'I love you, Lucas." I smile up at him.

"I love you my little peanut." I smile down at our daughter.

"I love you both so much," Lucas beams. "Nothing will ever come close to this moment." He smiles at me.

"WHEN IS THE WEDDING!" Caydence squeals with excitement. "Oh and I love you!" She says loudly.

"As soon as Mommy will allow," Lucas smirks. "Mommy's like to plan these things" he adds.

"Mommy can we do it tonight?" she whines.

"Honey, we have to plan it and get us both really pretty dresses and make sure everyone we love is there." I smile at her.

She is excited to have us both forever, that much I know.

"Lucas, time to suit up and get game ready," one of his teammates calls out. Lucas heads into the pit and we make our way to join our families in the VIP section Lucas got us.

The game starts an hour later and is going amazing. Lucas is incredible. They are winning and everything is wonderful. It is so cool to see him play again, and he is even better than before. He is truly a machine out there. No wonder The Giants were willing to lose two of their best to get him.

Our families are so excited. I finally take a second to look at the gorgeous princess cut diamond on my finger and sit in amazement that we have made it here.

I am tuning out our families and listening to Caydence who is in my mom's lap talking about all the things we should have at the wedding. Our proposal played on the big screen at half time, and we will be all over the papers tomorrow. All my dreams are coming true. Not the papers and media stuff and his wealth, but with the man I love. I look down to the field and that's when everything falls apart in an instant.

CHAPTER 26

(LUCAS)

She said yes!!! I am beaming. I feel like my whole body is coming alive for the first time since high school. She really said yes. She is mine forever.

All the guys are congratulating me, and I could not be happier. The man that has become my best friend, Johnny, one of our linebackers makes his way over and gives me a man hug.

After so long keeping everyone at an arm's length away, it is so amazing to have such a good friend.

"Dude, you did it. You got the girl." He smiles at me.

"I know, I am still on the high man." I respond with a smile.

"Don't go slacking off in this game now. We need you to win." He jokes.

"It's going to be the best game of my career, because tonight I am playing for them." Que the catcalling and name calling from the team. We may be grown men, but we still act like a bunch of high school jocks picking on one another, but tonight I welcome it. Nothing can kill the joy I feel. I got to place a ring on both of my girls' fingers and get to marry my dream girl.

We make our way out on the field, and I have to look insane because even with my mouthpiece in, I cannot stop smiling even while thinking about the pregame interviews were filled with questions about our engagement already and I was happy to brag on my beautiful family. I take a second to think back on the interviews.

"Lucas, when will the wedding be?" one reporter yells.

"Lucas, aren't you angry you did not know about your daughter? I get marrying her when you knocked her up but isn't it a little late for a shotgun wedding?" another asks.

"The wedding will be whenever my gorgeous fiancé wants it to be. As for the comments about shotgun weddings and knocking her up, I could not be prouder of our daughter, the wonderful job Maddie has done raising her and am so blessed to have the opportunity to marry my dream girl and be in my daughter's life after I ruined it the first time and no one will speak ill of them again."

I was happily bragging on my family until that asshole put in his two senses.

Dipshit.

Whatever, end of interviews, because I am not having that shit. Time to focus on the game.

It's just after halftime and we are up by ten. The first half went by in a blur. I am playing a damn good game. I have not missed a single pass and my teammates seem to be on the high with me.

I did not have this level of friendship with The Cowboys players and feel like each one of these guys are my brothers. It is amazing how much things can change in only a few months. I went from being a shell of a man who was only good for his skills on the field, to being engaged to the love of my life, with an amazing daughter, with friends and family by our side.

I am still reeling at the fact that my parents showed up. I called to let them know what I was doing, and they insisted on coming. After everything with my dad, I was shocked he even cared and even more shocked that I kind of wanted him here to witness me getting everything I wanted and everything he took away despite him.

Our video playing at halftime was amazing. I wanted to run into the stands and kiss my girl, but I couldn't. Proposing before the game was amazing, but on the flip side, I want to be with her right now so badly. My world is finally complete.

My head is bothering me slightly after a hard tackle, which should send off alarm bells and I am supposed to let my coach know, but this game is important, because I am playing for my girls.

It has been a long time since Maddie has seen me play and I want to make her proud.

I call the play and we get into position. I pull Johnny aside and let him know about my head. He will watch my ass the rest of the game.

As quarterback, a lot of the game rides on me. It's a good thing I am good under pressure and even better to have friends on the field by my side.

I throw the ball to my wide receiver, and he takes off for another touchdown. Before I even know what is happening, I am in the air. One of the players got past our defense and I am going to go down hard.

I have been here before and nearly died when my helmet flew off. It is like everything is moving in slow motion.

That's when I feel it, my helmet is slipping loose, because this asshole pulled on the strap intentionally. It comes off just before I hit the ground. Just before everything goes black, I see my girls faces, if this is it for me, I truly had it all. I hear Johnny screaming and know people are rushing all around me as I fight to stay awake.

All I know is that I am hearing and able to think, which is more than last time.

Again, I think of my girls and how much I love them and regret not speaking up about my head bothering me.

I finally have it all and my ego wanting to make Maddie proud tonight watching me play may have cost me everything. And with that thought, I see their smiling faces and then I go into the nothingness, and it all goes black.

CHAPTER 27

(MADDIE)

I can hear myself screaming. He just hit the ground without a helmet and is not moving. I know better than anyone how awful his last injury was and how serious this could be.

Without thinking, I turn to my mom who is holding a crying Caydence. "Baby, mommy has to go down there, I need you to stay with Nana so I can go check on Daddy okay?" I say as calmly as I can.

"Mommy I want to go with you!" She cries out. "Listen baby, Mommy has to go, but I promise to come get you as soon as I can." I say and jump up.

To my shock, Mr. Andrews is coming over to help my mom console Caydence.

I do not have time to dwell on that. I take off at a dead run, not caring who I push out of my way. I need to get to him right now.

I make my way down the corridor Lucas showed me earlier, burst through the doors and security is trying to stop me and I know I am making a scene and just do not care. Johnny, Lucas's best friend tells them to let me through.

I rush past him and out onto the field where they are loading Lucas onto a stretcher. I hear someone behind me, and Johnny is there with Victoria who I did not even notice has followed me.

They rush him off the field and I climb into the ambulance with him. Victoria is being held back and I ask them to please let her come and Johnny hops in behind her with his coach cussing at his departure.

"Breathe Maddie," Victoria's arms wrap around me. "He is strong, and he will make it through this." She says with strength in her voice.

"Victoria, get on top of the media. Here," I pass her my phone, "my logins are under notes and my passwords are his birthday. Log in as me and get the story out in a way that will protect him before someone else does." She takes my phone from me and gets to work.

"I am shocked you even thought of that. It is my job and I didn't." She states while continuing to work.

"Football means everything to him. Protect him." I state emotionless.

Johnny's hand reaches over to clasp mine. "You are his everything. Not football. He is fighting and going to make it through this for you, not the game." He says confidently which results in my tears breaking through.

He wraps his arms around me while I hold onto Lucas's hand for dear life. He has to wake up.

"Lucas, I need you to wake up baby. I need you to show me your baby blues and tell me everything is going to be alright. I cannot lose you, not again." I weep openly.

I feel Johnny's arms tighten around me and notice his eyes are glassy with unshed tears. He is trying to be my rock, and I so appreciate him, but right now all I want is to see Lucas open his eyes.

We get to the hospital at record speed, and they rush Lucas back and tell me I need to wait.

A kind nurse comes over and shows me to the waiting area in the intensive care unit. She brings me forms and I do my best to fill them out, but I am shaking uncontrollably.

Victoria and Johnny are here with me. A few minutes later, I am still trying to fill out forms when the rest of our families burst through the doors and Caydence runs towards me.

"Where is Daddy?" She cries out.

"Baby, they are back there trying to help Daddy get better. We have to wait for the doctor." I say trying my best to comfort us both.

My mom reaches down and picks her up. "I am sorry honey, there was no way she was going home and had to be here." She says with concern.

I do my best attempt at a smile, "I understand, Mom." I say.

Mr. Andrews approaches me and reaches out his hand, "Listen I can fill these out for you." He says in a comforting tone.

"Thanks, that would be helpful." I say quietly. "He was a shell of a person, Maddie. You brought him back to life and I am so sorry for everything I did. I brought this for you." He hands me a letter. "I should have given it to you when he asked." He says and turns to walk away.

"Mr. Andrews, I know you were doing what you thought was best, but I love your son. Don't ever doubt that again please." Is all I can manage to say.

It has been three hours and finally a doctor is walking our way. Thank God my mom took Caydence to get some food.

"Mrs. Andrews?" he asks. "I am his fiancé, Maddie." I state and wait.

"Are you aware that Lucas had a previous brain bleed that never healed fully?" he asks me.

"Yes." That is all I can manage to respond.

"Well, it is much worse this time. I was able to stop the bleed, but there is swelling in his brain. He has not woken up and to help decrease the swelling, we have placed him on life support so his body can rest and his brains swelling can go down and attempt to heal. I make you no promises, he is in a critical state, but I assure you, we are doing everything we can to save him." He is using a professional, practiced doctor tone, which leaves me feeling more hopeless than anything. I cannot even speak.

"Will he survive?" Johnny is right next to me, still in his full gear.

"I cannot say for sure, right now he is fighting for his life, but we have done everything we can and the rest is up to him." He states without emotion.

"Can I see him?" I blurt out.

"Yes, I will take you to him. We only allow two people in the room at a time, is there someone you would like to take with you?" He asks, this time with some compassion to his tone.

"Johnny." Is all I say in return.

I ask Victoria and Becca to inform my mom of what is going on away from Caydence and to send her back to bring Caydence when she returns to take Johnny's spot.

Johnny and I make our way to the room and when we enter, I feel like all the air in my lungs comes out in one huge gush.

There he lies, in a hospital bed, with more machines than I have ever seen attached to him and my heart crumbles to the floor. Johnny helps me to a chair and moves it right next to him and I reach down, and grab Lucas's hand tightly and openly weep while laying my head on his arm.

"Hey man," Johnny begins. "I am doing everything I can to take care of your girls like I promised you if this ever happened, but I am not you dude. I need you to wake up and come back because I am looking at your girls and breaking in half watching them break apart at the thought of losing you. I need you to wake up my man. Fight for them," He chokes on his words, "fight for me bro."

We hear a sound at the door and I see mom outside with Caydence.

Johnny leans in and hugs me. "Listen, I promised him I would take care of you guys if anything happened to him. I will keep that promise until my last breath, so I am not going anywhere, okay? I have someone bringing me clothes and things. I am here, Maddie." He finishes with a tight hug and then trades places with Caydence.

She is just young enough to not understand how serious this is, but just old enough to know it isn't good.

"Daddy, I need you to wake up for Mommy. I know, I need you too, but Mommy has never been this happy. You make her happy Daddy. Please come back to us, okay? I finally have you, don't leave me Daddy" She cries on his arm as I had been doing moments before and I know I have tears literally pouring out of my eyes.

"Caydence baby, I need you to go home with Nana. I promise to call you if he wakes up, no matter what time it is, but Mommy has to stay here okay?" I say as calmly as I can.

"I will go with Nana, stay strong Mommy and know I love you and so does Daddy." I hug her tightly and let her leave with my mom.

When she gets to the door I say, "Daddy loves you too baby and so do I."

One by one, all of our loved ones come in and speak to him and hug me.

I ask everyone to go home and rest and offer my apartment to his parents.

Johnny insists on staying with me. An hour or so later, Victoria comes back with a bag for me with clothes for both Lucas and me. I am not sure she ever truly clocks out of work, but today that is a good thing. She is more than his employee; she has become family to us all. I head to the bathroom to wash my face and change into sweatpants and when I come back out, Johnny is sitting in my place holding his hand. He moved when he sees me and silently moves to the chair in the corner. I appreciate his silence. I don't have it in me to talk right now.

Nurses and doctors come in and out all night. Johnny has finally fallen asleep on one of the cots they brought in for us.

Sleep will not find me again, until I know he is okay, that much I am sure of.

CHAPTER 28

(MADDIE)

It has been three days.

There has been no change beyond the swelling in his brain going back to normal. Doctors keep saying that it is up to him to wake up now.

He is no longer in a medically induced coma, but has not come out of the coma yet.

I am finally alone.

Johnny went to help with other family members and check on Caydence for me. I know I won't be alone long, so I pull out the letter his father gave me three days ago and decide now is the time to read it and hear from him in some way.

I slowly open the envelope and begin to read.

Maddie,

I know you hate me right now, but I hope you will read this letter and hear me out. First, I want to say that I love you, with every fiber of my being. I love you more than life itself and life is just not worth living if you are not in it.

Secondly, I want to say that nothing is going on between Kate and me. She came over and was mad about prom and me being with you as normal and was saying hateful things and leaned in and kissed me after I told her to leave. She must have seen you and got her bright idea to split us up, which is currently working, but I hope you believe me.

You are everything to me, Maddie. I was going to give up OU and follow you to New York even if it meant I would never play again. My parents did not take this well, so if my dad seems like an ass when giving this to you, that is why. I had signed the OU contracts, but I had not sent them. I changed my mind because you mean more to me than football ever will. I love you so much. I will walk away from the contract even now and end my career to be with you. I don't care about being sued or anything else. I just want you. Please call me. Please. I will never stop waiting by the phone. There is no one else for me Maddie. You are my forever and always. Please believe that. There is nothing I won't do to be with you and spend my life with you. I know we are young, but I also know that you are it for me. I love you with all of my heart. Please talk to me. I will wait for you until my very last breath, this I promise you.

With all the love in my heart,

Lucas

I finish the letter and am openly weeping. All those years and this letter says everything I have always know, he loves me and I love him.

All these wasted years when he was willing to give up everything for me. He would have been the amazing father he is from the start, and I ruined everything. No, his father did by not giving me this letter and Kate did with her lies.

He wouldn't even be in this bed right now. I can't even say that I would have let him give up everything for me, but just the thought of him not playing and this never happening has me feeling so angry.

"Baby, please wake up. I am right here; I haven't left, and I never will. I love you too and I need you.

I fold the letter up and put it back in my purse and as I am bent over, I see his fingers move. I immediately stand and start calling his name and begging him to come back to me.

I call for a doctor and one rushes in and confirms he is starting to wake up and encourages me to continue talking to him.

So, I do, about everything, about how much we need him, about Caydence, about how amazing he is, anything that comes to mind, I am saying aloud. "Baby, I love you. Can you hear me? Baby, Caydence is dying to see you. Baby, I love you so much. Come back to me."

Johnny wakes up and I tell him the news and don't even hear his response as we both continue to speak to him and beg him to wake up. "Dude, come on man, you are so close and have come to far and finally got the girl, you gotta wake up man." Johnny and I are talking in tandem, both begging his to wake up.

This is the first shred of hope since this all started, and I can't stop watching him.

He is moving around more and more, and they take off the breathing support and some other things I have no idea what they were doing. I continue to talk the entire time and praying silent prayers just wanting to see those beautiful blue eyes.

And that's when it happens.

They slowly start to blink, and I cannot help the sob that escapes me.

He tries to speak but has no voice. I scream for the nurse, and she comes in with water and begins to check his vitals.

"Sir, you were in an accident on the field and hit your head pretty hard." She says in a calming voice and does a series of tests.

The doctor comes in and examines him further. I can't take my eyes off his baby blues I was so scared I would never see again.

He finally speaks and looks at Johnny.

"Doctor, how long have I been in here?" Johnny looks at me confused.

"Baby, that's Johnny, your best friend." I say quietly. Still reeling at hearing his voice.

"Nurse, can I have some more water", he says while looking at me. This time, alarm bells are going off.

"Baby, its me, Maddie." I say cautiously.

"Can you tell me my name?" he asks.

Johnny rushes out of the room to find the doctor that had just left and I am left staring at Lucas.

"Lucas. That is your name. It's me baby, it's Maddie. Your fiancé." I say hoping it springs his memory and he is merely foggy from the coma. Doctors rush in and begin to ask him questions and take him for another brain scan.

When they return, they ask me to see them in the hall. Johnny comes with me.

"Maddie, Lucas is suffering from memory loss. He does not know who he is or have any memories of anything." He starts, and my heart shatters completely.

"He could get his memory back and this be short term, but he suffered a lot of brain damage, and may never get his memories back. We need to keep him a few more days and ensure he is stable, but the best thing you can do is take him home and resume normal routines and hope his memory returns." He finishes.

I know I am staring at him blankly and am in in shock. I am so thankful he is awake and alive, but he can't remember me at all?

"Is there anything we can do?" I ask still shaking.

"Like I said, the best thing to do is to get him home and in routine. Try to help his memory return, but unfortunately with brain injuries such as these, there is nothing else medically we can do to bring him back." He says sadly.

After a few minutes of processing, Johnny and I head back into the room. He looks at me like I am a stranger, but to him, he is a stranger too. Johnny and I sit in silence for a while with him.

"So, you're my fiancé?" he asks all the sudden.

"Yes, my name is Maddie. We also have a daughter who is five and named Caydence." I speak slowly and quietly.

"I am sorry I don't remember you guys. I can see it is making you sad." He says sadly.

"Hey, listen, the doctors want you to stay here a while longer, but then I can take you home and we can try to go back to normal and see if your memory can come back. Is that okay with you?" I ask scared he won't want to come with me.

"Yeah, that sounds good. I mean, I get to go home with a gorgeous woman, it could be worse." He chuckles and the sound makes my heart warm, but also ache.

Hours ago, I would have given anything to hear that sound, and now he has no idea who I am.

I don't know how, but I know even if he doesn't get his memory back, I will never stop fighting to make him fall in love with me all over again.

I will never give up on Lucas Andrews, the love of my life, ever again.

This may be the hardest fight of my life, but he has always sacrificed so much for me and I will not stop until I bring him back to me.

NOTE FROM THE AUTHOR

Maddie and Lucas's story has had a lot of bumps in the road, but their story is just beginning. Keep an eye out for Lover's Reborn, which is book two of their duet coming soon.

Do you think Maddie can bring him back?

Or do you think they have to start all over and fall in love a second time?

How do you think Caydence will handle all of this? What about his football career?

Do you think it is over?

There is so much more to their love story and more to come and I look forward to taking you on this journey with me. Thank you so much for taking the time to read this story. I hope you enjoyed these characters as much as I have enjoyed writing them.

SPECIAL PREVIEW OF
LOVER'S REBORN
(LUCAS)

I wake up, in a hospital of all places, have no idea who I am, or what is going on. Doctors are coming in and out, one nurse continues to call me baby, which is so weird, and I am rushed to complete head scans and tests.

Once I am back in my room, this gorgeous brunette is taken out and comes back in looking upset and scared. I can tell she has been crying. Supposedly, she is my fiancé, which is insane to me.

"So, you're my fiancé?" I ask with trepidation. I am not sure what to feel about this all. I didn't even know my name until a few minutes ago.

"Yes, my name is Maddie. We also have a daughter who is five and named Caydence." She is saying the words but looks so tired and broken and something inside me aches, because somehow, I am the one to blame, because I am the one that doesn't remember.

"I am sorry I don't remember you guys. I can see it is making you sad." I can hear the sadness in my tone, I may not remember her, but somehow the thought of her hurting cuts like a million razor blades.

"Hey, listen, the doctors want you to stay here a while longer, but then I can take you home and we can try to go back to normal and see if your memory can come back. Is that okay with you?" I can see she is scared to even say the words.

"Yeah, that sounds good. I mean, I get to go home with a gorgeous woman, it could be worse." I say with a laugh. I may not know her, but somehow feel like I do, and she may be the key to getting my memories back.

"Hey man, so what did you say your name was?" This guy is standing way to close to her and keeps putting his hand on her back, which makes me see red even if I don't understand why.

"I'm Johnny. I am on the team with you and am your best friend." He says and again he sounds sad too. Man, I don't know anything, but seem to be only causing people around her pain. So, this guy is my best friend. Wait, did he just say team? And why is he touching her back again.

What team? And can you stop touching her please?" I say annoyed. This is surreal. How do I remember nothing at all?

"Yeah, sorry man. You made me promise to take care of her if something went wrong with you." He sighs, but removes his hand, which makes me feel slightly better. "We play for the Giants. You are an NFL player." I can hear the pride in his voice and can't help but to feel proud of myself in this moment.

"Wow, so am I good?" I ask.

"Yeah man, you are one of the best quarterbacks to ever play and it is only your third season." He says and I can see he admires me and also see why we are friends even in just this short time with him.

"So, listen. I know you do not remember her, but our daughter, Caydence would really like to come see you. She has been so scared you wouldn't wake up." Maddie says with hesitation. "I understand if it is too much but needed to ask for her." She says with a sad smile. I know it may be too much, like she said, but if it might make her smile a real smile, it would be worth it.

"Yeah, that sounds good. The doctor said the smallest thing could bring my memory back, right? I would think seeing my own kid would help." I say and smile at her, which I don't plan, but just seems to be the effect she has on me.

"Great, she is here in the lobby. They were on the way before you woke up and have been waiting. I will go get her." She says and smiles, and it is the first real smile I have gotten since I woke up and it sparks something inside of me.

"I'll go get her." Johnny says and again, I find myself feeling bitter. Is this jealousy?

"Thank you." Maddie replies and hits him with a real smile too and that makes me boil, those smiles are mine. Woah, that's a strong feeling to have for a stranger. I am still reeling at my own thoughts when Johnny walks back in with a beautiful little girl with blue eyes that sparkle.

"Daddy!!!" She squeals. "I knew you would wake up! I know Mommy said you don't remember anything, but what about me? Do you know me Daddy? My Daddy said he would never leave me and I know you have to know me!" She is excited and so sure of herself, it makes me want to lie, but somehow, I do not think that is what I would normally do with her.

"I am so sorry peanut, but I do not know you either, but I want to remember, that much I can promise you." I say and try my best to smile and assure her.

"You will remember again." She says with such assurance that even I believe her and it gives me hope.

"You may not remember me, but I am going to come up there and lay with you and hug you and you are going to love it." She says and starts climbing up. Before I can even respond to her, Maddie cuts in. "Baby, why don't we give him some space. This is a lot for him." She says and seems so sad again.

"No, it is okay. I would like to hold you peanut." I say and have no idea why I keep calling her that.

"My daddy always calls me peanut, so you must really be him." She climbs up and snuggles into me. She smells like honey and lavender and it's so familiar to me somehow.

I may not know who I am, or who any of these people are, but somehow, I know this is where I belong, and it gives me hope that maybe I will remember someday.

Ashley Webster © 2022

Don't miss out!

Visit the website below and you can sign up to receive emails whenever Ashley Webster publishes a new book. There's no charge and no obligation.

https://books2read.com/r/B-A-CXYT-IUBZB

BOOKS2READ

Connecting independent readers to independent writers.

About the Author

My name is Ashley Webster and let's be real, I am a romantic at heart who dreams of romance and happily ever after – be it bright and sunny or dark and mysterious. I was born and raised in Texas and am truly a Texas girl at heart, even have a small southern drawl to match. I am single mother and if any of you are single moms, you know that all of your time is devoted to your kids, but my two girls are my life, and I would not have it any other way. You can find me curled up with a book almost every night, because not only is it how I like to spend my me time, but it is an escape from the dishes, laundry, dance practices and daily routines. All us moms need that right? You will also find me cheering my daughters on while they hit the stage as competitive dancers or spending quality time with those closest to me, because those people are why I am here today, and they mean the world to me.

I spent my early career working in business administration and finance, but that quickly bored me to tears and I hated going to work daily. I have always had a passion for writing. It was an outlet and a way to explore a different reality when life was not as shiny as I wanted it to be. I decided to go for my dreams and quit the awful (to me) world of business and dedicate my time, energy, and heart into creating stories you can get lost in, because I understand the importance of that.

After almost ten years working in finance and three business degrees I hope to never use again, I got the crazy idea to go back to school to master my true passion at Southern New Hampshire University. While working toward that, I earned a place in the International English Honor Society and the National Society of Leadership. I wanted to pursue a degree in creative writing so that I could better master my craft and show my daughters that it is never too late to chase your dreams and create your own happily ever after. It may not look like I thought, but it is the greatest choice I ever made for myself, and it has led me here where I can do a job I love and connect with awesome people like you. You can get to know me through my writing, because I promise you, I put my whole heart into every story I touch.

Read more at https://ashleywebster3.wixsite.com/ashley-webster.